AFRICAN WRITERS SERIES

Founding editor · Chinua Achebe

The Minister's Daughter

$$\frac{2}{3} \div \frac{3}{4} = \frac{2}{3} \times \frac{4}{3} = \frac{8}{9}$$

$$\frac{2}{3} \times \frac{3}{4} = \frac{2}{4} = \frac{1}{2}$$

MWANGI RUHENI

The Minister's Daughter

HEINEMANN
LONDON · NAIROBI · IBADAN · LUSAKA

Heinemann Educational Books Ltd.,
48 Charles Street, London W1X 8AH
P.M.B. 5205, Ibadan. P.O. Box 45314, Nairobi
P.O. Box 3966, Lusaka
EDINBURGH   MELBOURNE   AUCKLAND   TORONTO
HONG KONG   SINGAPORE   KUALA LUMPUR
NEW DELHI

ISBN 0 435 90156 7

Printed in Great Britain by Cox & Wyman Ltd.,
London, Reading and Fakenham

1

'Tell me, Grace, what does beer taste like?'

Jane Njeri had never tasted beer in her life.

'Do you mean to tell me that you have never tasted beer in your life? What kind of a girl are you? You better wake up and start living. Jane, you better be careful, otherwise you will die one of these days without ever having done anything in your life. The other day I saw a girl exactly like you who was knocked down by a bus. I do not know whether she died or not . . .'

'Just shut up for a while. The trouble with you, Grace, is that once you start talking, you just go on and on and on . . .'

'As I was telling you, Jane, this girl was about your size and she was knocked down by a bus for no reason at all. But she had the most lovely miniskirt ever seen anywhere. Her dress looked very expensive. You should have seen her wig. And the boys, those boys. They came straight out of nowhere and in no time they were helping her to get into a car which came straight out of nowhere as well. That is what I call a successful girl. I guess if you got knocked down by a bus and you lay down there throwing your legs up in the air, the driver of the next car would not even notice you. He would just come running over you and finish you up.'

'Why? I have red knickers on and not every good driver is colour-blind.'

'And what else do you have?' Grace was almost sarcastic.

Jane Njeri thought for two minutes or so. She had nothing else worth talking about. Her religious father Absalom Gacara had seen to that. Absalom Gacara is saved in the Lord. He walks in His light during the day. He walks in His light during the night as well.

Jane Njeri has been around for the last sixteen years. She has not come to Nairobi by mistake. She has come to stay with her uncle Gideon Murage for a very good reason. The Murages need domestic help very badly. Gideon's wife had a baby eighteen months ago. Then she had another baby three months ago. The maid cannot quite cope with all the washing and the cooking that has to be done in this home. That is why Jane Njeri is here. It is also during the December holidays. Jane Njeri will be doing her School Certificate next year at Tumu Tumu Girls' High School.

Grace Wangare has now stopped talking. She was interrupted by the wailing of this new baby. Grace Wangare is the maid in this household. She is very hard working. Whatever this girl does, she does it well.

Grace Wangare is shorter than Jane Njeri, a lot shorter. But a little older, too. She is a good eighteen years old. She is not at all bad looking. In fact, when she smiles, she makes a lot of men change their minds about her. She therefore spares her smiles until a proper moment comes. There is no proper moment for Grace unless there is a boy around.

Grace Wangare is the type of girl who has a prominent behind and a depressed front. She sometimes tries to straighten herself up but whatever she does, her things do not really like going flat. I do not see why she even bothers because her boyfriend Bethwell Mbarathi adores her the way she is. He says she looks different.

Wangare did her KAPE some time back and actually passed. She passed quite well. But her home is way behind Naivasha near those dark mountains that you see on your way from Nairobi to Nakuru. Her home is in fact somewhere near the top of one of those mountains. Quite near the clouds, in other words. Up there nobody knows anybody who knows the big people in high schools around Nakuru or elsewhere. Wangare did not go to high school. But she did the next best thing.

She tried her hand at various jobs in the farms. Picking pyrethrum, for example. Peeling potatoes for mummy. Sewing her old clothes. She got bored to death and so she came to Nairobi. The

Murages bumped into her by chance and so they employed her as a maid with no arguments at all. She gets ninety shillings a month with food and free housing. Grace Wangare saves ninety shillings a month and she has been doing it for more than a year.

Grace Wangare is a very broad-minded girl. She has no prejudices about things. She does not have a long list of do's and don'ts. She is religious, like all women are, but her religion changes with the weather. She likes good food and good clothes. She likes good company too. She has this boy at Makadara called Bethwell Mbarathi and another one who lives somewhere near Ngong. The Ngong boy is just a spare.

Kilimani Estate in Nairobi was built for people like Gideon Murage. He is a Marketing Manager with a very famous company. His wife is a Registered Nurse at the Kenyatta National Hospital. The Murages are rather fond of babies. Two kids in fifteen months is not bad going.

The house that the Murages live in is what people call a three-bedroomed bungalow. Everything about this house is just fine. But the bloke who put the bedrooms together made one big blunder. All the bedrooms are bunched together. This is a great shame. The parents sleep in this bedroom, the children sleep just next to them and the maid sleeps in the third bedroom just across.

Grace Wangare and Jane Njeri sleep in the same bed in this third bedroom. Once they lock themselves in there, you never know what they are doing. They remain awake for many hours and they are experts when it comes to keeping quiet. They are also experts at listening to whatever might be going on in the main bedroom. Did I tell you that the Murages are fond of babies? If you ever build a house of your own, make sure that one bedroom is at Ruiru, another one is at Limuru and the third one is way down at Athi River. This is my advice, and you had better take it while you can.

'Grace, you haven't told me what beer tastes like,' Jane says.

'Well, I'll tell you, Jane. The first time you taste it, you will not like it. It tastes something like raw banana skins mixed up with quinine. But after a while you forget the taste completely.'

'Forget the taste? And remember what?'

'You remember nothing, because it gets into your head. Then you want to forget everything.'

'Oh! Next Sunday we must ask for permission to go to church. Instead we shall head for Makadara. Your boy friend must buy us some beer. Next Sunday I will drink beer for the first time in my life. Grace, I am feeling very excited about all this.' Jane was really excited about it all.

The Murages are away at work and the children are asleep. Grace Wangare and Jane Njeri are determined to use their few minutes of freedom to the full. Before long they will be preparing lunch.

'Don't worry, Jane. Bethwell will buy us so many beers we will not be able to finish them. If he is broke, I will come to his rescue. I am worth a thousand shillings and if you do not believe me just look at my savings book.'

Grace opened up her box and showed Jane the little book. Jane stared at it as if it were Queen Victoria's diary. She had never seen a savings book before. The little book had figures all over the place but she could not see the magical figure of one thousand anywhere. But it was there. It was definitely there, I assure you. Grace is worth a thousand, exactly as she said. If you thought that housemaids do not have money, then you better change your mind.

'I have never seen a book like this one before,' Jane said.

'What else have you never seen before?'

'I have never seen a boy kissing a girl.'

'Don't worry, you will see this and more next Sunday. What else haven't you done before?'

'I have never worn a miniskirt.'

'I can lend you mine.'

'I have never used perfume.'

'I can lend you mine.'

'I have never put on stockings.'

'I can lend you mine.'

'I have never been kissed by a boy.'

4

'I can lend you mine. I have two of them.'

Jane Njeri had never done anything worth talking about, thanks to her parents. She had been brought up in a very strict manner. A clergyman's daughter does not grow up like other daughters. Definitely not like Grace Wangare. And when the parents happen to be saved in the Lord on top of everything else, life ceases to be life and becomes religion all the way. Jane Njeri knows what it is like growing up in a religious family.

She was born at a place called Ihithe sixteen years ago. Ihithe is a famous little place at the bottom of the Aberdares in the Nyeri District of Kenya. If you look in front from Ihithe, you see Mount Kenya right across at the end of the horizon. It is a beautiful view, especially at sunrise. But the people at Ihithe do not care much for mountains and scenic beauty. They have lived with these things all their lives.

Behind you at Ihithe there is nothing, just a forest. Beyond that there are the Aberdares. Some history teacher told me that these mountains were named after a white man called Mr Aberdare. He was the president of the Royal Geographical Society when another white man called Thomson was getting lost in Nyahururu looking at waterfalls. I think there is a lot of humour in the history of this country.

Ihithe can be very cold, especially in July. It can also be a very interesting place. Everybody here is either a brother or a sister. They are all very firm Christians and they are tied together by the bond of Salvation. They are all strengthened by the Spirit, and they rejoice a lot in His Name.

All this was started by a tall, dark fellow called Absalom Gacara. He was the first-born of his family. Gideon Murage was the last-born. In between the two there are many brothers and sisters, real ones this time.

Absalom Gacara first went to school at Ihithe and then Wandumbi. He did fairly well at school. He was extremely good at debating. He also excelled in Bible lessons. But he was not too happy with geometry. And his arithmetic was not at all nice.

When it came to dividing fractions, for example, he could never remember when to turn them upside down and when to leave them upright. But on the strength of his love for the Bible, he was chosen to go to Tumu Tumu for higher studies.

Which he did. Then somebody suggested that he could go one better and become a church minister. Which he did. In between matters, he met a girl called Agatha Waceke. She was short, with a fair complexion, and rather talkative. Absalom thought she was too romantic. At one time he even suspected that this girl had too large a dose of the demon in her. But he married her in the end. Agatha Waceke thus became a clergyman's wife, Bwana Absalom's wife.

Those who knew Agatha could not believe that she married a *Bwana*, of all people. Agatha was anything but the religious type. She was not moulded to fit into churches and her eyes were not made for reading the Bible.

But in this world unexpected things do happen. A surprise or two every now and then is a good thing.

Bwana Absalom was then installed as the minister at Ihithe with a very wide diocese. This extended to Gathuthi and Gatumbiro and almost swallowed Wandumbi. Bwana Absalom had a lot of sheep to look after. He also had a good share of goats.

All this was a long time ago. It was during the days of the famous Bwana Calderwood. It was during the time when the Church of Scotland was establishing itself in the Nyeri district. It was the time when Tumu Tumu was the only centre of higher learning for miles and miles around.

Agatha wanted a daughter. A first-born daughter is a great asset. She begins helping her mother with the cooking at the age of four. She goes down to the river to bring water at the age of six. She goes to the forest to bring firewood at the age of ten. By the time she is twelve, she can go to the market to sell maize, beans and potatoes. At thirteen, she begins bringing boys home with her.

Bwana Absalom, on the other hand, wanted a son. Everybody in the Bible started off with a son; God, to begin with. He would most

6

certainly be taught to say grace before meals at the age of four. From then on, he would follow the footsteps of his father. He might even become a minister of the Church at long last.

But Agatha and Absalom never got a son. They never got a daughter either. Years rolled by and nothing happened. Absalom comforted Agatha and said that this was the Will of the Lord. He quoted the Bible inside out in order to prove that the Lord chastises those He loves.

Agatha had different ideas. She consulted witchdoctors without her husband's knowledge. They told her that there was nothing wrong with her. She went to Mathari Hospital at the bottom of Githuuri Hill in Nyeri for a complete examination. She was told that there was nothing wrong with her. She went to Nyeri Provincial Hospital and she was told the same thing.

One day she told her husband that she was going to see the famous Nairobi Show. Instead, she went to see a famous gynaecologist. He gave her the longest medical examination that she had ever been through. And his verdict?

'There is absolutely nothing wrong with you, Agatha. You are a perfect specimen in every conceivable way. Absolutely fit for human consumption.'

'Then why don't I have a baby?'

'Because it takes two to have a baby.' This doctor could still remember what he read in medical textbooks a long time ago.

So Agatha came back home dejected. All she could do was to go on living, hoping that a miracle would happen. No miracle happened. All she could do was to listen to Absalom talking about the Bible and preaching in church.

And marrying young couples. Bwana Absalom married everybody for miles. It was twenty bob a time and he was not doing badly. He would exhort them to increase and multiply and fill the whole earth until there was standing room only. In other words, try and beat the rabbits at their own game.

The married couples would go away and do exactly that. In nine months flat, two people would become three. Some couples would be in even more of a hurry to obey this command about filling the earth. They would begin increasing a mere three months after marriage. Some people run while others walk, you know.

Absalom told Agatha that all those children at Ihithe were hers. He told her that it was much better that way than having only one or two children at home. He went on to relate that in Heaven they would have as many children as they wanted. It was cold comfort for Agatha, but there it was.

A little later, Absalom and Agatha became very interested in the new revival movement. This was a movement for salvation. It was a movement for reviving the spirit, strengthening the soul, rejoicing in the Saviour. This movement was spreading through the countryside like wildfire. It embraced many Christians. It brought the Spirit right to the people's doorsteps.

Bwana Absalom and his wife Agatha were soon converted. They were converted from sinners to children of God. It was difficult to imagine what sins they had committed previous to this, but they were now sinners no more.

Before long, Agatha and Absalom were the pillars of this new movement. They became its most vocal supporters. They sang and they prayed. They preached and converted others. They kissed and embraced every new convert.

They organised meetings and held large worship gatherings. They rejoiced in pulling people from the mud, as they put it, into the ways of the Lord. It was a new experience. They met a lot of people and made many new friends.

Still, Agatha could not forget that she had no child of her own. What frightened her was that she was getting on in years. Soon she would reach the point of no return. She thought about these things for many long hours.

Life for Agatha and Absalom was no longer dull and monotonous. There were always meetings and festivals to organise. There were a hundred and one people coming into the house and there was an equal number to visit in their own homes.

There was a lot of singing and rejoicing at these meetings. There

8

was a lot of embracing and kissing too. Quite often Agatha came home late.

Often they had to spend the night out at the meetings, singing and rejoicing with the other saved brothers and sisters. Often they would attend different meetings and come back home at different times.

Every few months or so, there would be a massive festival of the saved ones. The first was held at Ihururu. Others were held at Gathuthi, Huhoini and Wandumbi. These were gigantic affairs. They went on for days. The saved ones liked them. So too did Agatha, especially the evening sessions when everybody would confess their sins. When everybody would kiss and hug one another.

Everybody was above suspicion. Everybody walked in the Lord, not on their own two legs. Men and women intermingled freely yet nobody as much as raised an eyebrow. With the Lord and the Spirit, all was well.

Nothing could go wrong. Not even when Agatha felt unable to attend these meetings any more. She was beginning to get rather tired after doing very little. In the mornings, she would not feel at all well. She even found herself putting on weight, especially in one direction. This was a brand-new experience. Agatha was confined at home. But the meetings and the festivals went on.

And so it came to pass that Agatha one day gathered courage and announced to her husband the good news.

'Absalom, I am with child,' she said.

'Holy Lord be praised,' Absalom answered. 'I told you that He would not desert us.'

'Yes, indeed, my husband. His Name be praised now and always. He putteth the mountains down into the valleys, and the valleys he elevateth up to the mountains.'

Absalom was the happiest man for miles around. He would look at his wife and then at himself and then walk round the house in great contentment. He told everybody in his diocese that his wife was going to have a baby.

His sermons were now concentrated on holy wedlock. How husband and wife should live together as one person, body and soul. How it was wrong for brothers and sisters in the Lord to misuse prayer gatherings for their own selfish ends. How wrong it was to sleep away from home for whatever reason. How everybody should copy Agatha and Absalom in all their ways.

And so it happened that in the month of August, 1950, Agatha Waceke, wife of Absalom Gacara, was relieved of her burden and gave birth to a baby girl.

And what a baby girl this was! It was joy and loveliness all wrapped up in one. Very fair features, soft skin, even a little black dot on the cheek. Delicate lips and nice little ears. If Hollywood ever wanted a film star of no age at all, this was it.

Njeri was her automatic name. The first child of the Agikuyu is named after the father's mother or father. Absalom's mother was called Njeri. The girl's name had to be Njeri.

Saved brothers and sisters poured into Bwana Absalom's home like bees. They came in the morning and left at midnight. They held the child in their hands and they sang in jubilation and gladness of heart. Mother Agatha enjoyed every minute of it. It was a brand-new experience.

Many giffts were brought. The year had been a good one at Ihithe and the harvest was beautiful. The maize cobs were half as long as the hand and the beans were as thick as the thumb. The sweet potatoes were pushing out of the ground, causing many cracks below the sweet-potato tops.

Aren't people cynical? Apparently even when a person gets saved, he keeps his eyes about him. That is why an occasional brother or sister would comment on the baby's light features and then look at the father's very dark skin. But Absalom was not interested. He was the proud father of the most beautiful girl ever born.

On the eighth day the baby girl was baptised by a guest minister and called Jane. Daddy wanted the girl to be called Faith, or Hope, or Charity. He had every faith and hope that mummy would accept one of those names. But Agatha had no charity. She stuck to her guns and insisted on Jane. This was the one name she really liked. If she had been given a choice, she would have chosen this name for herself. When a woman like Agatha makes up her mind, no mountains or valleys can make her change it.

Jane Njeri, the little beautiful girl, was brought up in a holy family. There was the mother, first, the father, second, and the only begotten daughter, third. Jane Njeri did not grow up like other children. When a child is the only child in the family, that child does not grow up like other children.

Jane Njeri used the most expensive nappies, towels and soaps. Her pram was a showpiece, and for those who had never seen a pram in their lives the thing looked like a dream from the other world. This girl had the dandiest little dresses that you ever saw. A mosquito net was bought at Nyeri for her. This was a little superfluous because people at Ihithe do not know what mosquitoes look like.

Mother Agatha would go into fits if daughter Jane cried too long. Papa Absalom would order that the child be taken to hospital if it sneezed. There were two maids to look after this child. But only the mother would wash the child because she would not trust anybody else, whatever his colour, sex or creed.

People with a reputation for having evil eyes were not allowed to look at this baby. The maids had strict instructions to cover up the baby completely if one of those people of ill omen was spotted at a distance. At times, the baby was lucky not to suffocate in her own pillows.

People without babies of their own were of course most welcome. Mother Agatha would give them a lecture on how to get a baby even when all the odds are against it. She would show them the girl, pointing out that this was what a real baby ought to look like. Those who did not appear to be interested in these lectures or in the baby were turned out of the house.

After three months, mother Agatha claimed that her baby could speak. Not all the time, but at night when there was nobody else around to prove it. She insisted that this was the most intelligent baby ever born at Ihithe. Jane Njeri certainly looked pretty, but whether she had anything inside that lovely head of hers remained to be seen. Mother said that the baby was growing at twice the normal rate, as if she knew what the normal rate was. Everybody expected Jane to begin walking at six months.

When Jane ultimately began walking at the age of twelve months, mother insisted that there is not an awful lot of difference between six and twelve months. Before long, Jane was looking at Bible pictures. She could play with the Bible and even tear off pages from it. Daddy Absalom tried to show her how to say grace before breastfeeding. Jane was still breastfeeding. Mother Agatha was not one of those mothers whose main phobia in this world is being seen around with two drooping breasts. Agatha's were sucked for a year and over, yet they remained straight and aggressive.

The way this girl walked. The way she smiled. The way she rolled her eyes. All suggested that Ihithe was on the way to producing a beauty queen. All suggested that Ihithe had a girl of destiny, a girl whose future was unlikely to be free from intrigue, however protected she might be. And was she protected? Oh boy!

As Jane grew up in health and strength, she was taught how little girls say their prayers when they wake up in the morning and when they go to bed at night. How little girls sit down with their legs together, and with their hands on their knees. How little girls do not ask too many questions, unless it is about Ruth or Rachel. Above all, how little girls avoid little boys as fire shuns water.

Teacher Andrew Karanja is the greatest teacher ever born. He likes telling people about his olden days at Kahuhia and how he used to teach his own teachers. He also likes being where the action is. He is not yet the headmaster at Ihithe, but he likes calling himself the deputy headmaster. He goes even further than that. He does a lot of things that only headmasters are supposed to do.

Such as welcoming Absalom's daughter to school on the first day. He knew that Jane Njeri was coming to school long before anybody else did. This was going to be quite an occasion. Even Teacher Andrew Karanja himself was in for a few surprises.

Jane Njeri entered Standard One in great style. Not only did she have Teacher Andrew Karanja holding her hand, she was herself the complete pupil in every respect. Her parents were there, admiring her from a distance. Admiring the pink dress and the white shoes with white stockings. Admiring the beautiful black hair tied with a ribbon.

It was the first time in the history of Ihithe Primary School that a Standard One pupil was seen with a beautiful writing-case. If Teacher Andrew Karanja had known, he would have asked her to open it for the benefit of the other little children. Inside it, they would have seen a pencil, three exercise books, a fountain pen, a pencil sharpener, the Old Testament in pictures and an umbrella. An umbrella was necessary just in case it rained inside the classroom. It sometimes did.

Jane Njeri turned out to be extremely good in class. That beautiful head of hers apparently contained something apart from fresh air. As days passed, she grew taller, and those legs of hers grew longer as well. Within a few years, Jane was something worth looking at, even if she was still a child.

By the time she was in her fourth year at school, Jane Njeri was a force to be reckoned with. The teachers were extremely kind to her. Teachers are normally kind to good-looking little girls. But boys looked at her, then left her alone. This girl was beautiful, but she was the daughter of a clergyman. This was not the sort of girl that one played with. This was Absalom's daughter. The Minister's daughter.

Jane was more puzzled than anybody else was. She saw boys playing and joking with every other girl, but not with her. She could not understand why boys just looked at her and stopped at that. At times she felt very lonely and forlorn. Something was being denied her. She had not done anything wrong to anybody but she was not getting as much out of life as her classmates were. She could not understand what was wrong with her.

What Jane would never know in her life was that Teacher Andrew Karanja had been briefed by Bwana Absalom to watch over her at school and see to it that she did not get into evil ways. Such as standing close to boys, talking. Such as doing high jump or hand-stand. And was Teacher Andrew Karanja strict? He even saw to it that Jane swept the classroom when she did something naughty.

But a girl like Jane Njeri never gives up easily. She was just not born that way. She had her own way of making up what she appeared to lose. Any boy who was bold enough to smile at her would be well rewarded.

The first boy to get interested in Jane was a bold little boy called Lewis Maranga. He was a good four years older than Jane Njeri and well ahead of her at school. Maranga was an extremely shy boy. Nobody would ever have imagined that this boy could hurt a mosquito. But Lewis Maranga had a big heart, the heart of a lion. And he had an eye for beauty.

That is why one day he went near Jane, looked at her, and smiled. Just that. She looked at him with those eyes and smiled twice. Not once but twice. Maranga's dormant feelings were fired all at once. He looked for Njeri the following day all over the school compound during games and smiled again. She smiled back. That's what Maranga wanted.

Poor Maranga. He could no longer forget this girl. To make matters worse, he was doing KAPE that year. But maybe the two could go together. Maybe he could conquer the Kenya African Preliminary Examination and Jane Njeri at the same time. He was definitely going to try.

How? By buying a blue envelope. By buying a blue sheet of paper torn out of a writing pad. Ten cents for both of them. By writing a letter to Jane. Which he did. By reading it three or four times just to make sure that there were no mistakes in it. Which he did. By giving this letter to another girl with strict instructions to deliver it to Jane. Which she did.

Jane took the envelope only because this girl insisted that it was hers. It was not quite clear to her why anybody would insist on giving her an envelope. The only thing written on it was 'J.N.', nothing more. The other girls understood what this meant. It meant that the envelope was hers. Maybe they were correct. So she took the envelope, put it into her writing-case and forgot all about it. There were more important things to do, such as playing games and reading the Bible.

Jane Njeri went home that day as usual. She threw her writing-case on her bed, then went to the kitchen to make some tea and to help out generally with cooking and washing. Agatha always liked to see her one and only daughter carrying out the household chores. One day she would be doing this in her own home. She might as well start learning now.

Later on in the evening, Njeri took her writing-case as usual to the table in the resting-room. She lit her oil lamp and poured out all her books on the table. She picked up her arithmetic book and began doing her homework. She was definitely much better at fractions than her father was. She could divide two-thirds by three-quarters and get the answer at the back of the book.

Papa Absalom came in as usual to see how his daughter was getting on with her homework. He became even more interested in her work when he saw her playing around with fractions as if it was one big joke. But she ought to be more tidy. Why, for example, were all those books lying on the table?

'Jane, all those books. Why don't you put them inside your case?'

'Oh, yes. I was in such a hurry to start my homework.'

She begins putting them back. A geography book, a history book, a geometry book.

'And what is this, daddy?' She holds the envelope in her hand. She does not remember a thing about that envelope.

Daddy looks at the envelope and says nothing. Written on it he sees 'J.N.'. He snatches it from his daughter's hands and puts it into his pocket.

'Good, Jane. Put all those books back and keep the table tidy. I am going to read Psalm Twelve. Do you remember Psalm Twelve?'

Jane did not have to answer that question. Papa Absalom was already gone. He went into his bedroom. He locked it, lit his lamp, and looked at his envelope.

A nice blue envelope. There was 'J.N.' written on it. It could not mean Jesus of Nazareth, could it? No. Let us look inside. Nice blue paper. And a letter.

Ihithe Primary School,
P.O. Box NYERI.

My lovely angel Jane,

This is the boy who smiled at you yesterday afternoon. This is the boy you smiled at twice in return. My heart dies for you. Jane, I think of you day and night. I love you, Jane. I would like to kiss you.

Please do not show this letter to your father. Write to me and tell me something. Anything you want.

Love and kisses.

L. M.

Bwana Absalom read this letter twice, three times. He became dizzy and his eyes could not see properly. His heart was beating loudly inside his chest like the Ashanti drums. Little droplets of sweat gathered on his forehead. He had never imagined that his nine-year-old daughter was capable of this.

But he calmed down in a short time. This girl did not seem to understand what the envelope was all about, otherwise she would have hidden it somewhere. Jane is innocent, there is no doubt about that. Her only sin was to smile. She must learn how not to smile at boys.

Bwana Absalom goes and calls Agatha. He shows her the letter. She reads. She reads it again.

Agatha is feeling very proud within her. She is really feeling marvellous. Her daughter is growing into maturity at last. She is

16

worth looking at, smiling at, writing to. But Agatha tries not to betray her pride. She puts on a grim face because she has a duty to keep her husband happy.

'What do you think of this, Agatha, isn't it outrageous?'

'It is. We must see the Headmaster as soon as possible. Our daughter must not be distracted from her education by naughty boys.'

'We shall see Teacher Andrew Karanja, not the Headmaster.'

'Why?'

'Because I gave him this girl to look after. Has he gone blind or something?'

Teacher Andrew Karanja was sent for immediately. He was shown the letter. It was not difficult to find out who had written it. The only 'L.M.' with that handwriting was Lewis Maranga. It was arranged that his body would be whipped. Tomorrow. In front of his parents. In front of Jane Njeri. In front of the whole school.

Maranga's parents were informed of the crisis that same evening by Teacher Andrew Karanja. Either their boy would be whipped or else he would leave school. Now, with the KAPE on the way, whipping would be far better than expulsion. That is what Maranga's parents thought. That is what anybody would have thought.

And so it was done first thing the following day after the assembly. The headmaster introduced the motion. Teacher Andrew Karanja brought out the culprit and laid him on the grass. He administered ten strokes of the cane. Bwana Absalom would have preferred forty so as to maintain parity with the Bible. But after ten, Teacher Andrew Karanja was extremely tired and so he stopped. But he had enough energy left after the whipping to deliver a short speech. He said something to the effect that a boy who writes a letter to a girl has an overdose of demons and it is only the cane that can expel them.

Jane Njeri wept quietly all the way through. Agatha Waceke wept quietly all the way through. Bwana Absalom was nodding his head with every stroke. But father, mother and daughter never let each other know their internal feelings. The trinity kept their secrets to themselves.

But for the speeches, Jane Njeri would never have known what the fuss was all about. She knew she was the cause. Her girl-friends confirmed this to her later. This episode made a very deep impression in her young mind, an impression she would never forget for the whole of her life.

Lewis Maranga did his KAPE and passed with flying colours. The Principal at Kagumo High School picked him up like a hot cake. Lewis Maranga wrote to no more girls, not if their fathers were church ministers. Not if they had cousins or great-grandfathers who were clergymen. And whenever he saw a minister walking on two legs, he would go into reverse gear and run at great speed and hide in the nearest toilet.

Maranga did well in School Certificate. But he was not picked up for higher education. Perhaps he was not even interested in being picked up. He disappeared into Nairobi and got a job with the Kenya Beer Agencies, Limited. He was attached to the accounts section.

Jane Njeri was taught by Bwana Absalom how not to smile at boys. 'And if the demon tests you and you smile once,' he said, 'by no means should you smile the second time. Strengthen your spirit. Open your heart to the Lord. Become a new girl and you will never fall.'

Three years later, Jane Njeri did her KAPE. With so much protection from distraction, Jane had little to do at home apart from reading. She was also a bright girl in her own right. So she passed well. The Headmistress at Tumu Tumu Girls' Secondary School picked her up as if she was a blue chip on the stock market.

At Tumu Tumu, Jane Njeri joined the revival group. She was saved. She was converted. She refused to look at boys. She received many letters from them but burned them all. She helped to convert other girls. She helped to burn other girls' letters.

Occasionally she would remember Lewis Maranga and remember the old love. Jane Njeri conquered the demon in her heart and refused to fall in love with anybody. But she could not forget Lewis Maranga, however hard she tried.

This is December, the end of her third year at Tumu Tumu Secondary School. She will be doing her School Certificate examination next year. She is in Nairobi to help at her uncle Gideon's home. Jane Njeri likes helping.

Jane Njeri has never been in Nairobi before. Everything around here is very strange. The house, for example. Big stone house with three bedrooms. There is television in the house. But some of the things they show? Papa Absalom would not like to see them.

Often Jane Njeri goes near the road simply to look at people. To look at the latest miniskirts. And are they short? She looks at girls passing. And what would they be wearing? At Ihithe they would call them naked. In Nairobi people say that the girls are merely sniffing a little fresh air. If Bwana Absalom saw them, he would faint.

Jane Njeri has been in Nairobi for two weeks and she has been thinking quite a lot. Could all these people be wrong? Could she in her own way be the only one who is on the right path? Will God throw all the Nairobi people into his hot, flaming hell?

Jane Njeri had no rest. For one thing, Grace Wangare would not let her. Grace talked at length about her own upbringing. She talked about her parents, her early life, her religion. At first it was Jane Njeri who attempted to convert Grace Wangare to the ways of the Lord. But before long, the hunter became the hunted. Jane Njeri was intelligent and she could answer questions. But her answers were stereotyped and unsatisfactory. No wonder therefore that Grace Wangare soon took command of her. Her way of looking at problems was simple and practical. It was human and realistic.

Grace Wangare made a deep impression on Jane. She was a simple KAPE girl. But she had the brains of a professor. She had answers to everything, answers that made sense. She was at peace with herself. She did not keep asking herself those small nasty questions that Jane Njeri did. She was a girl to be envied.

Those first two weeks were the most important two weeks in Jane's adult life. She sensed a new kind of feeling in her heart, a feeling of adventure. A deep urge to go out and explore the unknown. A mysterious feeling that she was still a baby, still immature, still a novice in the art of living.

She experienced a deep hidden pleasure in doing what she knew she was not supposed to do. At first she was extremely afraid of this pleasurable sensation. Then she slowly accepted it and liked it. Now she was ready to go out and look for it.

A rebellion had started in Jane Njeri's heart. This led to a state of self-discovery. A new life was being born. A new person was emerging. Jane could now recall moments when she had had doubts about her religious life. She could recall past occasions when she had lain awake for hours, arguing with herself about the meaning of life and what went on in it. But these moments had quickly passed into oblivion. They had to be forgotten. They were too dangerous.

But now things were different. At Nairobi she could try to be herself a little. Grace Wangare was there to help her do it. The Murages were themselves very liberated people. This was not Ihithe. There was no Papa Absalom here. Jane Njeri saw a new light, the light of life.

Jane Njeri was now determined to look, to find out, to experiment, to soak in this new thrill of self-discovery, to explore the new wonderful world, and to do things like the other girls did. To feel, to love, to live.

Grace had promised Jane that tonight they would do some listening-in. This was Grace's favourite hobby, and she was determined to introduce Jane to it. Listening to what other people do, that was the hobby. Jane was not quite sure what Grace was talking about but she was ready to learn anything new.

That Saturday evening, Jane Njeri wanted to make sure that Grace had not forgotten her promise. Jane was determined not to lose anything interesting in life.

'Grace, don't forget what you told me. Today is listening-in day.'

'How can I forget, Jane? A girl like you has so much to learn that I would be failing in my duty if I did not teach you about the more interesting aspects of life. From what you have already told me, you could do with about five lectures on elementary sex. Your past life is very hollow indeed. You have missed a lot in life. I am glad you seem so ready to learn. I am . . .'

'Kindly shut up for a moment, Grace. Why do you think that today is a good day for listening-in? Yesterday I tried to listen but I could not hear anything. And what have we been trying to listen to, anyway?'

'That's what I mean, Jane. I am trying my best to teach you interesting things, and all you do is to keep doubting my methods. Well, listen, today is Saturday and he is sure to come home drunk. Does that mean anything to you?'

'No, I don't have a clue what you are talking about.'

'All right. You will know what I am talking about tonight. It will be like an earthquake, I promise you.'

'What will?'

'Just shut up.'

It was Saturday, the day for polishing the floor and cleaning the windows. The day for looking for the cobwebs and for spraying the cockroaches. Those cockroaches. Nothing kills them. Not even those aerosol sprays which claim to be able to kill every crawling thing under the earth.

Saturday night. The night Jane and Grace were waiting for. The two girls vowed not to sleep, however long it took Gideon Murage to come home. It did not take long. He came home drunk, as most men do on Saturday nights. He ate very little. The girls could hear him cursing the food.

Then he entered the bedroom, banged the door very hard and locked it.

The girls' whispers were very low. Nobody could hear them. Their ears were extremely sharp. They could hear the slightest sounds.

'I heard something, Grace,' Jane said.

'Shut up, you idiot. He is just throwing his shoes down on the floor.'

'I can hear something else.'

'That's nothing. He is simply getting into the bed.'

Then all was quiet. How disappointing. Was this going to be like yesterday? Maybe yes. Maybe not.

Long after everybody else was asleep, the girls were still talking in secret whispers.

'It is all over now, Jane. Did you hear it?' Grace asked.

'I didn't. Why didn't you tell me to listen?' Jane was rather angry now.

'I heard it all myself. You have lost your chance.'

Not quite, because Grace related the whole story in her own words. She demonstrated what they would have seen had they been allowed into that bedroom. Jane Njeri listened with great interest. But some parts of Grace's story sounded like Dutch to Jane.

'When I get married, Jane, I will not allow it too often. It makes one have too many babies. Some people have a baby every year, all because of it.'

'Do you mean to tell me that is how people get babies?'

'You are the greatest idiot this side of the clouds, Jane. How do they get babies at your home at Ihithe?'

'Definitely not the way you describe it.'

Before long, Grace was asleep. Jane remained awake for a long time. She was thinking about a lot of things. Before long she also dozed off and joined Grace Wangare in the blissful world of slumberland.

2

The following day was Sunday. The girls had great plans for this day. The Murages were going to be at home the whole day. Jane Njeri had already noted that these people did not go to church. They did not even talk about it. But the girls asked for permission to go to church.

Mrs Murage had no objections. 'You can go to church, but you better come back soon,' she said.

Grace Wangare had other ideas. 'After church we want to do a little shopping. After that I would like to take Jane to my aunt's home. She has been complaining all these days that I do not see her any more.'

'All right, but make sure that you come back today.'

'We will,' she confirmed.

With that, the two girls made a beeline for the door. Before long they were at the bus stop. This was going to be Jane's first ride through town and it was bound to be exciting. Her clothes, however, were not particularly exciting. Jane was wearing a cheap blouse and a cheap skirt. She had cheap shoes on with no stockings. But not many people noted all these cheap things. Before long they were riding down St Austin's road, in a bus. Here comes Muthangari.

'What place is that, Grace?'

'It is called a convent. There are lots of girls there who have made up their minds not to get married.'

'Oh, you mean it is a Roman Catholic institution?'

'Well, Jane, let me finish about those girls first. An idea just got into their heads that they want to stay single for the whole of their lives. No families, no children, nothing. Just a lot of prayers and that kind of thing. How would you like to be in there?'

'I wouldn't mind. But only for a few months. Unless you have been in there, how can you claim to know what goes on inside?'

Jane Njeri is a broad-minded girl by nature. She appears to be ready to look at both sides of any problem.

'Some of these girls sometimes run away, Grace, don't they?' Jane asked.

'Many of them run away.'

'And do they get married?'

'Why not? They don't leave anything behind, believe me.'

'And do they get children?'

'Do they get children? Why not?'

'How, Grace? How?'

'I showed you last night.'

Then there is a pause. The girls look out of the bus. Cars keep passing them as they speed towards the town. These cars look very small when viewed from the inside of a big bus. Now they are on Kabete Road, just opposite the orthopaedic clinic.

'And what is that there, Grace?'

'It is a self-service store.'

'How do you self-service yourself?'

'You go there and pick up what you want.'

'I see. I must go there one of these fine days.'

Seeing Nairobi from a bus was definitely a very enjoyable experience for Jane. And with a girl like Grace Wangare to do the explaining, life was just marvellous.

'What are these buildings on the left?'

'It is a kind of a hospital where they deal with bones and teeth. If somebody knocks your teeth off, they will fit you with new ones in that clinic over there.'

'New ones? Made from what?'

'I am told that the cheap ones are extracted from dead monkeys. The more costly ones are made from other animals.'

'Surely it is wrong to fix artificial teeth if God does not want you to have any.'

'Well, Jane, it is also wrong to put on shoes if you were born without any, isn't it? And who was ever born with shoes?'

'This is not what I mean ... but tell me where we are now.'

'Westlands. If your future husband is a rich man with a good job, he will probably live in this area. This is where you will be coming to buy ham and mayonnaise.'

'Ham and what? Anyway, I would not really like to live in this place. It looks like a forest. And look at all these people. How does one find his way home from a busy place like this?'

Grace laughs. 'Girls like you do not need to worry. There will be a lot of volunteers to show you the way home.'

Jane was not listening. She was looking far to the left. 'I can see a house across the valley.'

'A house, or houses? Which one?'

Jane pointed at the one she meant.

'Oh, that one. It is a Museum. All the old things are kept there. There are all sorts of animals inside. They even keep people's heads in that place.'

'They do? Whose, for example?'

'That famous chief who died a long time ago, for example. What do you call him, the one who comes from Nyeri or Murang'a or somewhere?'

'I don't know of any old chiefs. But how did they get his head? How did they know it was not somebody else's?'

'Oh, they have very learned people in there. I think they are called professors. When I was there a long time ago, they showed us this chief's head. Big white thing with teeth all showing. Next to it there was a smaller head.'

'And whose head was the smaller one?'

'It belonged to the same chief when he was a small boy.'

Jane laughed hysterically. Then she said:

'But look at that tall cylindrical building there.'

'Oh, that? It is called the Hilton.'

'Hilton for what?'

'I think it is just a big boarding and lodging place. I remember I went to such a place with Bethwell one day. Not a big one like that, but a much smaller one. I heard Bethwell say that we shall get bed and breakfast. I saw the bed all right, but never the breakfast.'

'Well, perhaps you should have demanded your breakfast before demanding the bed.'

'I agree. It was Bethwell's fault. He headed straight for the bed and forgot all about everything else.'

There were now far too many buildings to look at. Jane Njeri just looked around with her mouth wide open. Then they came to a bus stop which was full of buses. Too many buses. People were streaming out of them incessantly. Others were pushing their way into them in a disorderly kind of way. She did not like the pushing. She even saw one woman with a child fall down, get up again, and then literally fight her way into the bus. Jane Njeri liked to think that life is planned and orderly. But apparently this was not so.

They got into a Makadara bus and soon they were off. There were no more tall buildings to see. Just masses and masses of people in all directions, some pushing handcarts and sweating like hell, others with torn clothes lying idly beneath the trees on the roadside. There were children carrying water in home-made carts. Lunatics searching the dustbins for food. Hungry dogs dragging their bones as they trotted along. Hungry pedestrians with sunken eyes and with no desire to live but no wish to die. Not like Westlands, this place. There were far too many poor people here.

These things disturbed Jane Njeri's young mind. But she did not have long to think about them. The bus had now got to Makadara and Grace Wangare was already on the way out. This girl was in a hurry to get to wherever she was going.

Grace walked with authority towards the block where Bethwell Mbarathi and his friend Mark lived. She had been there before. Jane Njeri followed her timidly from behind. This was going to be a very exciting day for her. She was going to meet boys. She was going to drink beer. It will be the first time she does these strange things. What can be more exciting than that?

The boys at Makadara were waiting. And they were talking, especially Bethwell.

'Mark, the girls are coming today. Is everything ready?'

'Yes, Bethwell. I have orange-juice just in case the other girl does not take beer. I have beer and I have a little vodka. Grace is sometimes mad on vodka.'

'But tell me, Mark, why don't you want me to tell them your real name?'

Mark Methu, as he preferred to be called, was a quiet young man, rather shy, but very fond of good company. But he had one great fear. He did not want to make any girl pregnant. He had seen his own brother's education interrupted because of this. Just to guard against his being entangled if something unexpected happened, he preferred to be introduced to girls under all sorts of names. Such as Mark Methu. Or Joseph Kariangwachi. But never by his real name.

Bethwell Mbarathi, on the other hand, has always been Bethwell Mbarathi. Tall, like a horse. Brusque, like a sailor. Exactly what Grace Wangare has always wanted. They are great friends, these two. I would not be surprised if the two got married before the year is over.

Bethwell and Mark live in adjacent rooms in a big block at Makadara. This block is divided up into six living-rooms. There is a common toilet and a bathroom. There is also one little gate for coming in and going out.

The boys' rooms are connected by a door which can be opened if the occupants so decide. This is a convenient arrangement. A married couple can use the two rooms as one dwelling-place. Two bachelors like Mark and Bethwell can go across to talk to each other so long as they are on good terms. These two are on very good terms.

Bethwell Mbarathi now gets out the letter that Grace Wangare wrote to him. He goes quickly over it, mentioning the most important points. 'My dearest Bethwell . . . we shall be at Makadara before ten o'clock on Sunday ... I am bringing my friend Jane Njeri with me ... she is young ... she is raw ... she is rather stupid ... get her a friend to keep her busy .. perhaps your neighbour will not mind ... I hope his girl-friend Eunice will not come when we are there ... I am longing for your kisses ...'

Then he whistled. 'Just listen to that, Mark, this girl of mine is tops.'

'Bethwell, how did a bloke like you get mixed up with a maid? A fellow with an Advanced Certificate like you should really look for something with class. A housemaid? You couldn't get lower, could you? Unless you went for a barmaid.' Mark was almost sarcastic.

'Now, Mark, shut up before I flatten you with that bottle of beer under your bed. Grace Wangare is my girl first and a maid second. Do you follow?'

'I don't. She is yours the day you marry her, not before. The day you get married to a maid, that is the day I shall laugh.'

'O.K., phoney Mark. Your Eunice does not have very much of a shape. She also should take a few lessons on how to cook. Have you ever tasted a dish prepared by my Grace?'

Of course they were joking. Bachelors like joking. They have an acid sense of humour.

Their two rooms were virtually identical. A bed in the corner. A curtain which could be drawn so as to conceal the bed. A table on the other side. A small cupboard with one or two spoons, one or two plates and one cup with a saucer. There was the immortal radio. There were one or two odd books. There were two or three sexy pictures on the wall.

But on this occasion there were the drinks as well. There were also a number of drinking-glasses. There were two more plates and two more spoons borrowed from somewhere. Somebody had made sure that there was a bag of charcoal outside. There was also a radiogram with a few records.

The floor was immaculately clean. There were no bits of paper on it. The beds were very well made up and the sheets were crisp and snow-white.

When the girls are coming, it is a good practice to hang out all the costly suits for them to see, and the ties. Bethwell and Mark did not live on charity, and they wanted to make this clear to their visitors.

'Tell me, Mark, are you excited?'

'About what?'

'About this new girl? She may turn out to be a killer. A little change is good for the soul, you know. Where is Eunice?'

'She went to Uthiru yesterday to visit her sick mother. Just as well. I hope she doesn't come back too soon.'

'To visit her sick mother? She's probably locked herself up in a small room in a hotel with a tall guy with an American degree.'

'Now, shut up. Don't talk like that. You know I am here this morning simply because you requested me to be. Hello. What's that?'

Somebody was knocking at the door. Very gently and very softly. Bethwell opened the door slowly. There was his girl Grace Wangare. She produced her special smile. This was the time for it. Bethwell smiled back. Then he looked behind Wangare and what did he see? A real beauty. Tall, cool, with very kissable lips. He promised himself not to look at this girl for too long. Grace might catch him doing it. He led the visitors into the house.

'This is Mark Methu,' he said. Then he waited for Grace to do the introduction.

'And this is Jane Njeri,' she said.

The girls sat on the chairs at the table. Mark was now in a slight state of confusion. He told himself that he was born a very lucky boy. Just look at this girl. Look at her. The cheeks look like ripe tomatoes. The eyes are like those of a doe. He kept glancing at her from a distance.

The boys had arranged that one of them should sit with the girls while the other one prepared things. Bethwell Mbarathi was the one to sit with the girls. This was a good thing, because he was the more talkative.

'What is the latest news, Grace? How are the Murages?'

29

'Doing well.'

'And the journey?'

'No hitches.'

'Jane, where exactly do you come from?'

'I come from Ihithe. It is way back near the bottom of the Aberdares.'

Now hear that. Mark Methu virtually jumped up into the air. He had a good reason to be surprised but he did not tell anybody about it. Bethwell continued with his cross-examination.

'And where do you go to school? I am sure you are at school somewhere.'

'I am at Tumu Tumu. I am doing School Certificate next year.'

Now Mark interrupted. 'Shall we take some tea?'

Grace Wangare had other ideas. 'Have we come all the way from Kilimani Estate for tea? We left a lot of tea behind.'

'Bethwell, would you like a beer?' Mark was definitely a little disorganised.

'I would like four beers. Can't you count?'

It was rather early in the morning but nobody appeared to object. For Jane Njeri this was just great. The moment had at last arrived. She was going to taste beer for the first time in her life. Jane Njeri was not the timid type. She was looking forward to the new experience. Everything looked great in this place. There were boys. There were drinks. Everything here was what she had always wanted.

Mark Methu placed four beers on the table. He placed a clean glass next to each beer. He kept looking at Jane through the corner of his eye. Then he opened the girls' beers. Then his. Then Bethwell's.

Bethwell's beer frothed and poured over. He snatched the bottle and quickly directed the froth towards his mouth. The frothing came to an end but Bethwell just went on sucking from his bottle. His Adam's apple kept rolling up and down as he swallowed and swallowed some more. His eyes kept opening and shutting with each gulp. This was a real he-boy. And a very thirsty one too.

Jane Njeri wondered why her beer did not froth out of its bottle like Bethwell's. Hers did not look like a real beer, or did it? And the drinking, what were the glasses doing there? She remembered having seen a few people at Ihithe drinking beer. They did it Bethwell's way, straight out of the bottle.

Mark now poured the beers into the glasses. Jane's first. Then Grace's. Lastly his own. Jane saw hers frothing a little in the glass. This was good.

Mark, the Master of Ceremonies, almost forgot his duty. He took up his glass and was on the way to helping himself when he remembered something. He growled, 'Cheers!'

Bethwell howled 'Cheers!' and did his round of knocking the other three glasses with his bottle. Mark did likewise. Grace came up with her 'Cheers!' and almost knocked down Jane's glass in her enthusiasm to show her that she had been through this before. Then everybody looked at Jane. But this girl was no fool She did exactly what Grace did and everybody laughed and cheered.

Bethwell was half drunk by now. He had gone through half a beer in no time. Mark gulped half a glass at one go. Grace took a mouthful, then put the glass down.

Jane Njeri took one big gulp and closed her eyes. Was this thing bitter? It was like a mixture of banana skins and quinine all right. At first she felt like spitting it out through the window. But with all those people looking at her, it would have been rather uncouth. So she forced herself to swallow the liquid. She was very relieved when it all went down.

She had a pang of remorse for a fraction of a second. She had already drunk beer. This was an evil thing to do. It was the best way of inviting the devil. Drinking beer was wrong; Papa Absalom had said so. But Jane had already reached the point of no return. She was a different girl now. She was no longer a coward. No longer afraid to see life as it is. This was a different Jane Njeri.

Bethwell Mbarathi was the ruffian in the place. He kept making jokes about drinking out of bottles. How much better it is than drinking out of glasses. How a little amount of beer goes a long way if taken that way.

How drinking in the morning is so much better than drinking in the evening, especially if the girls have got to go back. How before long everybody would be making a noise as loudly as empty tins.

Jane, for one, was not feeling like talking. This beer was making her stomach hot. Her eyes were getting dry and hard. Her head was feeling blank and stupid. Every now and then she would belch out a lungful of a very nasty gas. But beer she was going to drink. Come what may, she was determined to finish this bottle.

Above all, Grace was there, and she was drinking quite steadily. Her bottle was now almost empty. And was she enjoying Bethwell's jokes? But she herself was very quiet. Grace is like that, very quiet when she wants to be quiet.

At last, the two girls finished their beers. Then they looked at each other. It was obvious what they both wanted to do. They both went out to the toilet. The boys now had a moment or two to talk.

'Mark, listen to me. Our good beer is just about to be poured down into the sewer,' Bethwell said.

'I know, there will be a deluge. Have you ever seen Nyahururu Falls during the floods?' Mark laughed to himself.

'When they come back, give them something else. We have something else, haven't we?'

'Yes, we have. And when do we begin dancing?'

'You can have my Grace today. I want to keep to the new girl,' Bethwell said.

'Go to blazes, Bethwell. The new girl is mine. I am telling you Bethwell, this girl is mine. One of the best things I have ever done in my life was to come here today.'

The girls came back. They were talking and they looked cheerful. They were also a little drunk. Tall, beautiful Jane Njeri. Short, stocky, charming Grace Wangare. They were out to prove to themselves and to others that life does not consist in scrubbing floors and washing dishes.

'Mark, give the girls something better than beer, will you? We will keep to beer ourselves if you don't mind.'

Mark Methu disappeared through the connecting door into the other room. He made two vodkas with ginger ale. He was good at mixing drinks. He knew, for example, that girls like something sweet. He therefore tasted the drinks just to make sure. Then he brought the drinks to the girls.

'This is better, Jane, much better. Just taste it,' he said. Jane tasted it. It was sweet and nice. Then she took a gulp. And another one. Grace did the same. The two glasses were empty in minutes, Mark Methu went and replenished them.

The atmosphere was now relaxed. Everybody was talking at once. Bethwell, of course, was ahead of everybody else. Occasionally he would place his hand on Wangare's chest. Or sit on her thighs. Or pretend to kiss her from a distance. These antics amused Jane. The more she became amused, the more Bethwell would maintain the fun.

Mark Methu is a great calculator. Just at the right moment, he produced a record player out of nowhere. He put on a record and the whole place was filled with good, throbbing, rhythmical music.

Bethwell pounced on Grace, put his big hands at the back of her knees and raised her right up. He even brought his long mouth near hers but she bent her neck the other way. In the process, Wangare's miniskirt became even more mini. But he soon put her on her feet and began dancing with her.

Mark now moved the tables and the chairs to one corner. He approached Jane rather gently, compared with what had just taken place.

'May I dance with you?' he asked.

'I don't know how to dance,' she said.

'Do you know how to stand up, for a start?'

'Yes, I do.' What a question, she thought.

'Then stand up,' Which she did. Bethwell Mbarathi was looking back at her across his shoulder. This embarrassed Jane a little but she was now in no mood to care.

'Do you know how to walk? The way you walk to the classroom, for example?'

'Yes, I do,' she said.

'Then walk.'

Jane walked. From here to there and from there to here. Mark Methu walked along with her. Before long they were walking all over the place. Bethwell and Grace were quite amused at first but they soon concentrated on their own intimate dancing.

Music played and Mark saw to it that it kept playing. He was now dancing with Jane, holding her. Her dancing was not at all smooth. When a girl dances with a boy for the first time, she looks awkward. Occasionally, her knee would get caught up in Methu's legs. Methu did not mind, but she did. Sometimes her legs felt heavy and she would go out of step. In fact, Jane Njeri began wondering whether dancing was as much fun as she had been led to believe.

Bethwell was now high. So too was everybody else. Jane was feeling a little dizzy but quite happy. Bethwell dragged Grace into the other room and locked the door. Mark and Jane were left alone. They too stopped dancing, but the music went on.

Jane was relieved to see this dancing coming to an end. She went and sat on a chair in a corner. Mark came up with her drink and his and sat next to her. He was extremely enchanted with this girl. But he had to be careful. This was a strange girl. She looked extremely beautiful. His experience had taught him that beautiful girls are not that simple-minded. They have complicated life histories. They often come to know things which other people do not know. That is the story of beautiful girls, according to Mark.

'And what are you in Nairobi for, Jane?' he asked.

'I am staying with my uncle, Gideon Murage. I am helping them at home until the end of the holidays when I go back to school.'

'What will you want to do once you finish school?'

'I really do not know. Maybe take a job like you. Where do you work?'

'I am an accounts clerk with the Kenya Beer Agencies. It is a very large company which distributes beer to all parts of the country.'

'I don't think that I even know your other name.'

'Methu is my name.' That was a lie, a big one. There is nobody on record whose name is Mark Methu.

'And your home area?'

'Nyeri. Mathira.' That was another tall lie. Phoney Mark did not come from Mathira.

Mark now moved closer and put his hand around Jane's back. The palm of his hand rested on Jane's chest. Jane did not seem to mind. She sighed and sighed again and then looked at Mark. He looked at her and said nothing. All he did was to move closer so as to make it more comfortable for Jane. He pulled her a little closer to himself. He had a vague idea that he knew this girl.

'Tell me, do you like Tumu Tumu?' Mark asked.

'I like the studies. The teachers are very nice,' she answered.

'But Tumu Tumu is a long way from Ihithe, isn't it?'

Mark now began unbuttoning Jane's blouse. He removed three buttons and left the other one in place. He had no particular plan in mind.

'What are you doing that for, Mark?' she asked.

'I don't know. I guess I am getting interested in you.'

'But Grace told me that you have a girl-friend called Eunice. Is that true?'

Mark did not say anything. He buttoned back Jane's blouse slowly. Jane began wondering why he was retreating. Perhaps she should not have mentioned this girl called Eunice. Perhaps she had better keep quiet just in case she says the wrong thing again.

Mark removed his hand from Jane's back and excused himself to go to the toilet. The record player was now quiet. Nobody appeared to want any more music.

It was afternoon now and Jane was feeling rather hungry. But she did not care much for food. She was a little dizzy because of the drink but she was not caring much about anything.

Mark came back and knocked at the little connecting door. 'Stop it now, let us go,' he shouted.

'Go where, Mark?' Jane was wondering whether there would be any point in going back home this early.

Bethwell and Grace now came out from their room. Grace went and sat next to Jane. The boys went outside to arrange something or other. The girls utilised this chance to talk in whispers.

'How was it, Jane?' Grace asked.

'How was what?'

'Him. Is he romantic?'

'Is he romantic? He virtually disappeared with my blouse.'

'Oh, and what else? Did he take you to that bed?'

'For what?'

'Don't you remember what I told you last night?'

The boys now came back and the girls switched themselves off.

Bethwell was still in very high spirits. 'Is everybody ready to go out?' he asked.

Grace thought that somebody was playing them a trick. 'Go out to do what?'

'Don't you worry,' Mark said. 'We have a little surprise for you.'

The girls did what they were told. They gathered themselves together and straightened their dresses. Bethwell locked the room and led the party to the back of the house.

There was a good, clean Volkswagen car waiting there. It was Bethwell's car. Methu's blue Mazda was also there. But they were going to go in the Volkswagen.

'Get in, everybody, get in.' The girls were a little amazed at all this but they obeyed without question.

Grace went in front. Mark and Jane sat in the back. Before long, Bethwell was driving towards the town.

For Jane Njeri, everything was marvellous. Here she was, sitting in the back of a car with a boy. A romantic boy. His hands were around her. Sometimes the palm of his hand would be on her chest. Sometimes he would remove it from there and put it between her knees. Jane liked it. She did not object.

36

They went by an unfamiliar route and ended up near the Kenyatta National Hospital. Then they took Ngong Road and kept going. Bethwell drove right on towards Karen and then towards Ngong.

'Who doesn't know Ngong township?' Bethwell asked.

'I don't,' Jane answered.

'Here it is.'

'This? Just this?' Jane expected to see a much bigger town than this.

Grace Wangare was worried about other things. She had a boy who lived near there. She was hoping that he would have taken this day off to go to Gilgil or Nanyuki or some such other place.

Before long they were climbing a very steep hill. They were heading for the Ngong Hills. Jane Njeri loved every moment of it. It felt like an adventure story straight out of a book.

When they came to the top and got out of the car, Jane just looked in front of her and marvelled at the wonderful view. The expansive wasteland. Unspoiled, just as God created it. So different from towns. So different from Ihithe too. She had heard of scrublands at school but she had never seen one before. And the Maasai huts. But what did these people drink? Where were the rivers in this place?

They removed things from the car and went off in different directions. Mark and Jane took their things up a little hill and ended up under a tree. Mark spread out a blanket. He unwrapped a barbecued chicken and produced glasses from somewhere. There was a small bottle of vodka and a good number of ginger ales.

The chicken was good. It was washed down with a good helping of vodka. The two talked about the Rift Valley, the Maasai and the drought. After the food and the drink, however, Mark changed the subject to more personal matters.

'Jane,' he said, 'I know you. I have known you since you were a child.'

Jane looked up like a person who had been awoken from a dream. She kept staring at Mark as if he had an artificial nose.

'You only met me today,' she said. 'You have never seen me before, have you?'

Mark was ready to talk. But just to make the atmosphere more cordial, he gently persuaded Jane to lie down flat on her side. He laid himself flat beside her and put his hand between her knees. His other hand went round Jane's back. A little uncomfortable for Jane, but tolerable nevertheless.

'I know that your home is at Ihithe. I have been there once or twice.'

Jane could not possibly believe this. Still, maybe Mark was trying to get at something.

'I am trying to get at something, Jane,' he said.

'Yes, the way your hand is moving up leaves no doubt about that whatsoever.'

Mark said nothing. He was thinking how best to approach the subject without arousing any suspicion as to what his intentions were.

'Jane, your father is Bwana Absalom Gacara, isn't he?'

Now Jane raised up her head and looked at Mark straight in the eyes. She sobered up for a moment or two.

'Yes, you are right. This is very strange.'

'What is?'

'The fact that you know my father.'

Something else was also very strange. Mark is an expert with his fingers. They kept crawling up and this threw Jane into a perfect state of confusion. Jane did not know what to do. She took two or three minutes to decide on a course of action. Then she pulled out that hand and released herself from Mark.

'Shall I tell you something else, Jane?'

'What?'

'You are a virgin.'

'And you?'

'I am an explorer.'

'Then that's your last trip. So you know me then. Tell me how. I am really burning to know the explanation.'

Her mind was still in a state of confusion. She was trying to digest far too many things all at the same time.

'Surely you remember Teacher Andrew Karanja don't you?' Mark was now enjoying himself.

'Yes. He taught me for a long time. Are you his cousin or something like that?'

'No, teachers do not beat their cousins. That teacher gave me ten strokes of the cane for writing a letter to a girl. A girl called Jane Njeri.'

It all dawned like daylight. It was now as clear as the clear waters of the cold streams of Ihithe. All that Jane could do now was to open her mouth and stare at Lewis as if he were made of mahogany.

'You are Lewis Maranga, then?' she asked.

'Yes, I am,' he confirmed.

Jane looked at him in total bafflement. He resembled Maranga, he could be Maranga, he is Maranga. She just looked at him with her mouth wide open. He pulled her closer to him. She was glad to come. Their lips met and soon they were lost in a deep embrace. A long, long kiss. Then a sigh.

This was the most emotional moment in Jane Njeri's life. If this boy was Lewis Maranga, and there was every possibility that he was, there was every reason for shedding a few tears of joy. Which she did.

'I don't believe you, Mark. I don't think I believe you.'

This was not true, because Jane had no doubts at all who he was. Mark took out his wallet and produced an identity card with his photograph in it. He threw it at Jane.

'There, look at that. Read the name.'

She gazed at this card as if it was the first card she had ever seen. The picture was him. The name was Lewis Maranga. This was the boy she had always wanted to meet. The boy she had always promised herself would be the only boy she would ever fall in love with. And here he was. Here, indeed, he was, chatting away happily as if he had no care in the world.

'After Ihithe I went to Kagumo. But it is all over now, education I mean. I have a reasonable job and my main interest now is to get married and have a family.'

She listened and said nothing. Now she regretted that she had allowed herself to be so free with this boy. She should not have allowed him to unbutton her blouse. She should not have allowed him to put his hand on her chest. Above all, this other hand should not have been allowed to do whatever it did.

Maybe it was not too late for Jane Njeri to behave herself. Maybe it was not too late for Jane Njeri to be a good girl. Maybe it was not too late to show Lewis that she was not a loose girl. So she pulled herself away from him. She straightened out her clothes and sat down. From now on, things must be different. Lewis is not like the other boys. He must be kept out in the cold. He must be treated like a prospective husband.

Now that Lewis Maranga had let the cat out of the bag, he was prepared to relax and gaze out into the great valley down below. The great dry, enchanting valley.

But Jane was still puzzled. 'Shall I call you Mark or Lewis?'

'Whichever one pleases you more.'

'I will never call you Mark again,' she said.

'But why did you not want me to know your name from the beginning? Were you subjecting me to a test?'

'No.'

'Yes, you were, and you have succeeded. I am the most careless girl that you have ever met ... aren't I?' Jane began weeping quietly.

There was now a little natural tension between Jane and Lewis. They were no longer strangers. The carefree atmosphere had vanished into thin air.

'You still haven't told me why you didn't want me to know you at the beginning,' Jane said.

'Boys have always been tricky, Jane. I must apologise. I really didn't want to play you a trick or anything like that. Believe me, I didn't know you until after we met.'

'And Bethwell Mbarathi. Is that his real name?'

'Yes. And a hell of a Mbarathi he is, too.'

Lewis wanted to reduce the tension. He talked a lot about their early days. About life at Ihithe. About strict parents. About getting saved in the Lord. About old-fashioned Christianity.

Hours rolled by easily. It was now obviously getting late. It was time to go home. They woke up and bundled up their things. They went downhill towards the car. Bethwell and Grace were already sitting inside, talking.

'Mark, why did you take so long?' Bethwell asked.

'I am no longer Mark, I am Lewis Maranga. As I have always been.'

Bethwell understood. Before long the group was on its way back to Nairobi. The girls were dropped off at Adam's Arcade at their own request. Grace Wangare wanted it that way. It was getting dark, but perhaps it was too early to show up at Kilimani Estate yet.

They went to an ice-cream bar near by and sat down. They got themselves two large ice-creams and began licking them.

'Ice-cream is good after vodka,' Grace said. 'It makes you sober up quickly.'

'I am already sober, Grace. Do you know that boy? The one calling himself Mark?'

'Bethwell told me that this is not his real name.' Grace Wangare does not believe in keeping secrets.

'His real name is Lewis Maranga,' Jane said. 'I have known him for a long time. Grace, I cannot stop myself from falling in love with Lewis.'

'I see. He is romantic. The very shape of his face shows it. But what did he do to conquer you so soon? Are you so easy to convince?'

'Grace, I will tell you about Lewis Maranga one day.'

'How was it otherwise? Did he kiss you?'

'No. What did you say? Yes. And you?'

'No.'

'You locked yourselves up for a long time at Makadara.'

41

'We were just talking.'

'I was listening. Now I know how to listen. I am now quite good at it. Grace, you are a good teacher, you know.'

'And what did you hear? Don't forget that I was also listening.'

'Then it all cancels itself out. Grace, are you in love with Bethwell?'

'Yes. I always have been.'

'Grace, I am joining you. I am in love with that other person.'

'The person who almost ran away with your blouse? Any other juicy story?'

'Tell me yours first,' Jane insisted.

Grace told her story. Jane told hers too. One story was more detailed than the other. Wangare's.

The boys, also, were far from being quiet. On the way home, Bethwell talked a lot. Once they got home, they sat down to finish the beers which had been left over during the day.

'What are your impressions of this girl called Jane?' Bethwell asked.

Bethwell was hoping for a favourable answer. But this is not what he got.

'Awful. A beautiful girl like that is bound to be hopeless. I have never seen anything as loose as that girl. No morals, no principles, nothing. Must be due to bad upbringing.'

'But she is your villager. You should fall for her in a big way.'

'No, never. I have Eunice and I do not want anything more attractive than that. Bethwell, this girl's shape is a killer. She smiles like an angel. But she does not have the slightest regard for good behaviour. You know me, Bethwell, I am a strict person.'

'But you grew up together, didn't you? You know each other fairly well, don't you? The foundation is there. If I were you, I would think more about this girl Jane Njeri.'

'But you are not me. Correct?'

'Well, well. Lewis, is there anything good in this girl?'

'Yes, she is a virgin.'

'How did you find out?'

Lewis Maranga, the explorer, raised up his pointing finger, the way they do at political rallies.

3

Jane Njeri went back to Ihithe after her stay at Nairobi was over. In a few days she would be going back to Tumu Tumu to begin her final year. Bwana Absalom and Mummy Agatha were very happy to see their daughter looking so well, so cheerful, so healthy. Bwana Absalom, in particular, was very eager to hear from his daughter.

'Tell me, Jane, did you learn a lot of things in Nairobi?'

'Yes, papa, I did. I saw a lot of new things.'

'Such as what?'

'I saw a place called a convent. I saw another place called Westlands. And there was that tall cylindrical building called the Hilton.'

'Hilton? What's that one for?'

'For people who have nowhere to sleep. They have beds there and they give people breakfast.'

'We are intending to build something like that at Nyeri. Some of the people in towns are so poor that we have to feed them and give them somewhere to sleep. Tell me, Jane, did the Murages treat you well?'

And so they talked. Two people living in two different worlds. Two people unaware of what was going on in the other's mind. Mummy Agatha had her own questions too.

'Jane, how old is this new baby of Gideon's?' Agatha was still interested in babies.

'I would say about three months.'

'And how old is the other one?'

'About a year or so. Mummy, how come you did not have a baby after me?'

A difficult question, this one. But Agatha Waceke had to say something.

'Babies are not so easy to get, you know. I told you when you were a child that babies are bought at Karatina and it is a long way from here.'

'Well, mummy, I no longer believe in that story.'

'Why?'

'Because it is not true. You know that it is not true.'

And so they talked. Like mother, like daughter. They were both wiser than either of them thought the other was. They knew more than they were ready to tell.

It did not take Agatha Waceke long to find out that her daughter Jane was undergoing a tremendous change. The way she dressed, the way she talked, the way she kept her box permanently locked up. The way she was getting absent-minded so often. Like a girl who was thinking about a boy. Like a girl who was falling in love.

Jane Njeri went back to Tumu Tumu. She cut out a lot of her religious activities. She was really not very interested in this thing any more, but it was not possible to put an immediate stop to it all at once. People would get suspicious. Teachers would ask questions.

Studies were getting harder. Or it could be that Jane was finding it more and more difficult to concentrate, all because of Lewis Maranga. Jane was thinking about Maranga instead of thinking about algebra. She was thinking about Makadara and the Ngong Hills instead of concentrating on the life and death of the amoeba.

She had doubts about her feelings at first but in the end she accepted it all. She was in love with Lewis Maranga. She was in real love for the first time in her life. She was happy about falling in love with Lewis. Of all the boys, this is the one boy she would have liked to be in love with more than anyone else. She had told herself so a long time ago.

Now she could speak the same language with the other girls at school. Now she could talk of her boy. Now she could tell her own adventure stories. Now she was a human being, a person with her own individuality, a person who did what she wanted rather than what she was told. Life was sweet, marvellous. There was hope, there was reason to live.

Except for one thing. This girl called Eunice, whoever she was. Why did Eunice get attached to Lewis before she did? How could Eunice be requested to leave her boy? Jane's boy? If only Eunice knew of the long history that existed between Jane and Lewis. Jane cursed Eunice in her heart a thousand times.

Jane promised herself not to worry too much about Eunice. She liked to deceive herself that something would happen and Lewis would be hers one day. Love is blind, it has always been.

Jane Njeri wrote many imaginary letters to Lewis Maranga. She told him that she loved him. She told him that she was not a loose girl as he might have thought. She told him that when they met she was a baby, a big baby, a baby who could hardly tell the difference between a boy and a girl. She sealed some of these letters in envelopes and locked them up in her box. Maybe one day she would show them to Lewis Maranga. Maybe.

Jane Njeri went back to Ihithe during the April holidays. Bwana Absalom would not let her go to Nairobi this time. Mummy Agatha would not have minded but she wanted somebody to help her with the planting and the cultivating.

It rains cats and dogs in April. At Ihithe there is no flat ground and little streams gather all over the place. The footpaths become slippery. Women with loads on their backs occasionally take a tumble as they struggle to walk uphill towards home. Little boys enjoy sliding on the mud and they enjoy the occasional fall.

The little rivulets with sparkling water in them turn brown. But they clean themselves very quickly if the rains stop for a day or two. Maize and beans show up in the gardens immediately after the rains start. They grow up in a hurry and within a few days all the gardens which were covered with brown earth take on a new green look.

The boys who graze their goats near the gardens have to be careful. One goat can easily wipe out a whole garden in a short time. They like the young shoots. Every season, somebody's garden gets wiped out by a herd of goats or by a stray cow. The owner of the animal has to compensate the owner of the garden. The local headman has to decide on the amount of the compensation.

Jane Njeri was glad to go back to school for the second term. There was far too much work to do at home. Besides, Jane was now becoming aware of the fact that soon she would come to the end of her schooldays. Maybe she would continue with higher education. Maybe she would go and look for a job. It all depended on how she fared in the School Certificate examination. Just two terms left, and the new life would begin.

Before Jane Njeri came to Nairobi, a few interesting things had already happened. They were all centred on this girl called Eunice Wangeci.

Eunice Wangeci is a very charming girl, as everybody knows. She has rented herself a room at Ngara. This room is situated on the upper floor of a block of shops owned by a very rich man called Maina Menyu. A man who is always laughing. He laughs very loudly even when there is absolutely nothing to laugh about.

Eunice Wangeci's home is at Uthiru. She was educated there before going to Alliance Girls' High School, Kikuyu. She did not do particularly well. She obtained a third-class School Certificate. But this did not worry her one little bit. She did not want to do any more studies. She was not all that young to begin with. She wanted to see what life in the outside world looked like. Eunice has always been interested in finding out about life.

She studied typing and shorthand for a whole year. It was a hard course. But she did better than many girls. She passed her typing and shorthand at the first trial. She applied for a post which was advertised by a bank, and got it. She now works in a big bank on

Government Road. And what could be better than that for a girl of nineteen years?

One could call Eunice a tall girl with an oversize chest. She has rather large eyes and a little sharp mouth. She has good, long, black, natural hair. Still, Eunice sometimes wears a wig. A fashion is a fashion, and Eunice Wangeci is never left behind when it comes to fashions. And this is why Eunice is so different from many other girls.

Fashions. Good dresses. A delicate taste for cleanliness. Meticulous care not to look shoddy in public. No wonder Eunice looks even more beautiful than she is. She works hard to keep herself on top. Can't compare her with a girl like Jane Njeri who hardly knows how to put on a decent pair of socks. But then, if Njeri had mud all over her body, boys would still run after her. She has plenty of natural beauty. That is what Jane has that Eunice doesn't have.

Eunice Wangeci liked her job the very first day. She was assigned to work for Mr Munyi, a senior loans manager in the bank, whose office was upstairs. Mr Munyi's secretary was away on maternity leave so Eunice was taken on as a relief. But she worked well. She was kept on.

In the normal course of her duty, Eunice Wangeci had access to a lot of private bank accounts. Accounts of big companies, accounts of small firms, private individuals' accounts, the whole lot of them.

When there was not much work to do, she would ask for the bank statements of the big shots whom she knew. A good dirty hobby, no doubt. But Eunice enjoyed it. And there was this accounts clerk downstairs called Thuo Thenge. Very helpful. Thuo would show Eunice whatever account she wanted to see. She was really amused by some of the things she found out. She found out that all those big names you hear about do not have the fat sums of money in the bank that they say they have. That lots of them are at loggerheads with the bank manager because of non-payment of debts. That many unknown fellows have fat sums of money lying in the bank.

For example, this young man who comes to see Mr Munyi so very often. He has pots and pots of money in this bank. She knows his name, that was not difficult to find out. But who is he? Rather short, stocky, and very intelligent-looking. And his account? Oh boy, it has a lot of money. Too much money for one person.

What shall I, Eunice Wangeci, do? I have a boy somewhere at Uthiru, but I do not care much for him. There is not much in that boy. No big name, no big position, no title, no money. Just two legs and a lot of ordinary things in between. I wish I could get a boy like this one, this one with a fat account. But maybe he is married. Maybe he has a girl-friend. But he wears no ring on his finger. This is cold comfort though, because many married men do not wear rings these days.

What shall I do? I shall play the boss a trick. I must find out more about this young man. This is the sort of man I have been looking for ever since I was born.

'Excuse me, Mr Munyi. Who is this young man who comes to see you so often? The one who was here yesterday morning? He looks like a boy who was at school with me at Uthiru. Could he be the same one?'

Mr Munyi is very obliging. After all, how do you know whether your own secretary will not come to your aid one day? Above all, this has nothing to do with loans, just a little personal affair.

'This man is an accounts clerk with the Kenya Beer Agencies. He is an ambitious young man and he puts his money to good use. I don't think he is more than about twenty-two.'

Eunice Wangeci thinks: I am very lucky. I know his name. I know where he works and the name of his company. I know now that he is an ambitious young man. I know that he is not more than twenty-two. This may be the boy I have been looking for the whole of my damned life.

I must be patient. Patience conquers all. Next time this boy comes to this office, I shall do something. I shall definitely do something. I shall not just sit here and see him go in and see him go out. I will do something that day. Oh, when will the day come?

The day came. It was bound to come sooner or later. He walked in. She smiled instantaneously, effortlessly. The sweetest smile she was able to fabricate. And the most killing. No man on two legs could have failed to notice it.

He went in, talked to the loans manager, came out. He looked at the secretary. She smiled again. He smiled too and left. Was that the end? No, she followed him from a distance. She saw him get into a car. A blue Mazda. She noted the number, then went back to her office. There was shorthand waiting and it all had to be transcribed.

But shorthand can wait for a while. Eunice took up the phone.

'Is that the Kenya Beer Agencies?'

'Yes, can I help you?'

'Can you put me through to Mr Lewis Maranga?'

She knew he was not in. He could not have got back to the office so soon.

'He has gone to the bank.'

'Oh, I see. I have a cousin of his here who is looking for him. He says he would like to wait for him at home. Where is Maranga's home?'

The answer was loud and clear. Makadara Road, block so and so. House so and so. And if Maranga is not in, ask for Bethwell Mbarathi. They live together. And who is speaking? Clunk, Eunice cuts the line. Lewis Maranga got the message when he arrived at the office. He went home for lunch as usual. But there was no cousin of his at home. Only Bethwell Mbarathi. Well, maybe this was somebody else's message. People make mistakes, you know.

The following Sunday Eunice Wangeci went for a stroll towards Makadara. She knew the road and the house number. She knew the car. It did not take her long to find out the place. She looked at the house again and again. She looked at the blue Mazda car outside. Inside that house there was a boy she was very much interested in. A boy with a very fat account in the bank.

Eunice Wangeci is not quite the harmless girl she always appears to be. When you grow up at Uthiru, which is only a few miles from the country's metropolis, you come to learn a lot of things very early. Uthiru is not Ihithe.

Well, Eunice Wangeci did what Jane Njeri would not have dared to do under the same circumstances. She did not go and knock at the door. No, she did not do that. She did the next best thing. She went and knocked at the window. Well, almost. Because she went and stood at a spot where she could be seen from inside the house. The boys saw her, of course.

'Bethwell, I see a girl.' Maranga was quite excited.

'And the girl sees you.' Bethwell now looked out and saw the girl.

'She looks familiar, Bethwell. I could swear that I have seen that girl before somewhere.'

'Maybe she is the one you saw at the bank the other day. Did she look like that?'

'Could be. Quite possible. Yes, she is the one.'

'Lewis, if I were you, I would take a stroll in that direction. Then I would just say "Hello" casually. I would ask whether I could be of use. I would ask where I last saw her. I would ask her whether she can come in for a cup of tea.'

Lewis Maranga did exactly that. He went to the girl and said, 'Hello, I seem to have seen you somewhere.'

'Yes, I work at the bank. I work for Mr Munyi, the loans manager.'

'Oh, yes. Now I remember.'

The conversation went on. Before long Eunice Wangeci was sitting in a room at Makadara. A very talkative Bethwell kept Eunice busy talking.

Eunice charmed the two boys with her wit and good behaviour. Extremely polite and well cultivated. Very well dressed and extremely elegant. But she did not stay for long. She did not intend to. Her mission had been a success beyond her wildest dreams.

The boys took her to a bus stop and said good-bye. Then they came back to their rooms.

'Lewis, that girl is high class.'

'Yes, quite a long way from your Grace Wangare.'

'And quite a long way from you too. A secretary stenographer? A dictaphone typist? A palantypist-in-chief? Leave me to my Grace.'

'Grace the housemaid.'

'Yes. And if you think you can get that girl, you are deceiving yourself. You are just a clerk, remember.'

Lewis Maranga is not the sort of person to talk to like that. He has always had an eye for competition. Besides, this girl was getting into his bones. The secretary with the loans manager in a bank could be a very great asset. She could tell you a lot of things that you did not know before. She could tell you a lot about money. Lewis wanted to know a lot about money.

That is why he rang up Eunice Wangeci the following day. One thing led to another until they made a date. Saturday after work. He would collect her at the bank and take her to Makadara. It would be a good Saturday, this one, because Bethwell Mbarathi would not be in. The place would be as private as the bottom of the sea. That Saturday, Lewis drove his bird to Makadara.

'Move in, Eunice, this is where I live. A simple bachelor's place, that's all.'

Eunice moved in and sat down on a chair at the table.

'It is a very nice place, Lewis, I must say. How much do they charge you for it?'

'A hundred and thirty shillings.'

Eunice Wangeci's main point was comparison. She paid one hundred and fifty shillings for her room in Ngara. Hers was much bigger, more comfortable and perhaps even better furnished. She began wondering why a man with so much money should choose to live at Makadara, and in such a room. Lewis Maranga was definitely a mystery to her. This made the thrill of being associated with a man like this even more gratifying.

It was now about two o'clock in the afternoon. Lewis was definitely prepared to entertain his girl-friend. He mixed some vodka and ginger ale and put it on the table. It was a very well made drink, exactly what one needs to enliven the proceedings.

'Sorry, I don't take vodka.' Eunice was adamant. She was not going to have any vodka.

'Are you sure, Eunice, you don't want any?'

'Yes. I have never tasted it and I do not think I am really prepared to taste it for the first time.'

'Fair enough, and what about this?' Lewis produced some beers. He had quite a few types to choose from. He had a good knowledge of beers because he worked for a beer company.

'I am so sorry, Lewis, I should have told you that I do not take alcohol. My parents are very strict about it and it is my wish not to take alcohol until later in life.'

Lewis Maranga was now quite puzzled. He looked at this girl. Not all that beautiful, but extremely elegant and well behaved. With a very good sense of dress and general make-up. Above all, with a mighty chest. Lewis Maranga falls easily for that kind of thing. But Eunice was proving difficult to please. Too difficult.

'Then what shall I give you to drink?'

'Have you got Sprite?' Which is a kind of a soft drink.

The answer was No. Lewis had to rush to the shop to look for it. He came back with half a dozen bottles and opened one.

Eunice tasted it warily at first as if she was suspicious that somebody might have put alcohol into it by mistake. It tasted soft, very soft, and sweet. So she took it approvingly.

'Eunice, tell me about yourself.'

She talked about her strict upbringing. About her very religious parents. About her own strict ways.

Lewis Maranga was surprised with himself because he was getting rather impressed by this girl. He had not been able to meet many strict girls in Nairobi. Maybe this was an authentic specimen of the good, strict, sensible, sober and homely type. There are not many girls like that left in Nairobi any more. Maybe Eunice Wangeci is the last one.

The next item on the proceedings was a record player and a few records. The sound was good. It made Maranga's vodka go down more easily. It made him more dizzy, more drunk. Bold, like a lion. He approached this girl and asked her to dance with him.

She stood up but very reluctantly. She insisted that she did not really know how to dance. But she danced all the same. Not very well, but not very badly either.

Lewis Maranga was now quite merry. He was enjoying himself tremendously. So much so that he would occasionally pull Eunice right up to him. That chest, he wanted it closer.

'No, don't dance like that, Lewis. It is not right.'

This girl must have a very high sense of self-respect, or whatever it is called. Why won't she allow Lewis to do a simple little thing like that? All boys and girls do it when they are dancing. But perhaps Eunice Wangeci is different. That is why Maranga was not going to allow Eunice to go. No, not yet. She merits a little more study. A much closer understanding. She could be a girl worth thinking about, seriously. After all, this is how a bachelor meets his future wife.

The next item on the agenda was a little drive. Towards Ngong Hills, of course. Where else do you go to? Maybe it is more private up there at Lodwar or Mandera, but that's for the tourists, not for the locals.

There were a good many things in the boot of Maranga's blue Mazda. Blankets and pillows and drinks and a chicken. A very well done chicken.

On the way, Lewis tried one or two simple tricks. Such as looking for the gear lever between Eunice's knees. Such as opening the window on Eunice's side while making contact with that chest with his hand. Eunice frowned on these tricks. This girl was different.

She was even more different up on top of the hills. She kept to her soft drink. But she did not mind the chicken. She sat on the blanket and would not recline. She kept her knees together and kept both hands on top of both knees. When Lewis tried to un-button the blouse, he was virtually thrown down the cliff. That's how it went.

And when they went back home, things were no better. Lewis Maranga was all worked up. He was now beautifully drunk. He locked his little house and hid the keys. Then he tried to keep Eunice busy. He played the records. They danced a few steps. Then he brought out something to eat. He kept looking at his watch. The night was slow to come, but it came all the same.

At half past eight, he stopped the music. He drew the curtain that kept the bed from view. He directed Eunice towards the bed. She just looked at it and went on sitting at the table.

'Let us go there, Eunice. There is always a first time.'

'No, Lewis, I have already done far too many things for the first time.'

'Such as?'

'Coming here, dancing with you, driving out with you. I need time to digest all these things. I am more interested in the future than in the present. I have also got my religious beliefs.'

'So too have I. But there is no future without the present. So come on, let us go.'

Eunice shook her head. Lewis now became a little brutal. He went and removed her shoes.

'You can keep those so long as you leave me alone,' she said.

'I will never leave you alone,' Lewis said. This was saying quite a lot.

Eunice was touched by this sentiment. She appreciated it. This is what she came for. She came to be seen and to be appreciated.

'Then don't go to bed alone, Lewis, let us sit down here for the whole night.'

'No, Eunice. I will respect your feelings. You are more to me than just a day's companion. I will make you your own bed.'

Did you hear that? Eunice was now feeling great. Something was now happening. Something she liked. The rich boy was getting interested in her.

Lewis now opened the little door that connected his room to Bethwell Mbarathi's. He prepared Mbarathi's bed nicely and asked

Eunice to go and sleep there. He gave her back her shoes. She went and slept there. Maranga slept in his own room.

Lewis Maranga could not sleep easily. His imagination would not allow him. What if he woke up and went to the other room? Is Eunice a deep sleeper or is she not? And what would he do if he got there?

But he decided to be a good boy, especially as Eunice had been such a wonderful girl the whole of that day. He took a gulp of vodka and slowly dissolved into slumberland.

Both were very cheerful the following morning. They parted amid great laughter and merriment. A foundation had already been laid for a deep, emotional love. There were more dates. There was more dancing. There were more trips to Ngong Hills and to other places. They went to the shows together.

But the atmosphere never changed. It was exactly what it was on the first day. Eunice Wangeci was strict and she wanted things to remain that way. Lewis wanted it that way too. This was his future wife. This was the way courtship ought to be conducted. Lewis Maranga was happy that at last he had found a girl he could say for sure was the proper girl to marry.

There is a little comfortable place somewhere along Kimathi Street. This place is called the 'Three Swallows'. It is very new and very modern. When you get to the door, you do not know whether to push it or pull it. It is a sliding door, and not many people know about it.

But Ali Kamau does. This place is his second home. He is in there every week-end. And he is never alone. How can a man like Ali sit there alone like a fool drinking cool beer all by himself? And what about all those girls you see moving forwards and backwards in Nairobi? The ones who wear minis and wigs? The ones who make their eyes very black and their lips very red? The ones with big ear-rings and tight clothes around their chests? These are the girls that Ali Kamau likes.

Ali Kamau has always been a kind of a mystery. But he is an enchanting fellow. He tells everybody that he grew up in the

Majengo slums of Nairobi but he managed to find his way into St Peter Claver's School and then to Mang'u High School.

It is on record that this man went to Makerere and obtained a Bachelor of Arts degree of the University of London. It is also known that after working with an oil company for a short time he went to the United States on a scholarship and graduated with a Master's Degree in Business Administration from the University of California. He is now employed by a local bank. He scrutinises business accounts and things like that. He also likes some of the girls who work in that bank. Especially the high-class secretaries. You cannot blame him, can you? A bachelor must be given time to look round. He must be given time to make a few mistakes before making the final mistake of his career, plunging into married life.

This was Sunday evening. Make it about six. Ali was gazing at his beer at the 'Three Swallows.' Sitting with him was this girl. She was sucking vodka and ginger ale. And liking it too. Because to-night she was the property of a top guy. A big fish. With two degrees and a fat job. Ali Kamau is no small man.

She was very well dressed, top to bottom. A wig up on top, a short mini down below. Very dark eyes, I don't know how they manage to make them so dark. A tight sweater around the chest. This girl must have done some geography when she was in high school. She knows all about hills and valleys, about projections and contours.

The 'Three Swallows' is always a little dark and you cannot see everything. But what you see is just enough. For example, that these two are not very sober. That they know each other fairly well. That this is not their first meeting by any means.

Ali breaks the long silence. 'Where were you yesterday? I came to Ngara at about this time but found your place locked up.'

'I thought I told you that I was going to Uthiru.' Which was a lie.

'Forget it, Eunice, forget it. I never live in the past. Let us thank your Lord for giving us another day to enjoy ourselves. Have something more to drink.'

That's the trouble. That's the trouble with Ali. That's why this two-degree bachelor never saves a cent. But Eunice knows all about him. She knows how much money he has in the bank. They work in the same bank. He does not have an awful lot. But he is an extravagant spender. And what is wrong with helping him to spend it?

'Ali, do you ever think of getting married?'

'That's a good question, Eunice. But it is a little too direct. Put it in a less direct manner and I will give you an answer.'

'Well, here it comes. Are you likely to fall in love in the foreseeable future?'

'Yes, tonight. What could be more foreseeable than that?'

'Naughty. But I really do think that you should think a little more about the future.'

'Who told you I don't, Eunice? As soon as I am reasonably well established in my job, as soon as I have a little house of my own, as soon as I have a better car, as soon as I have a little farm out there at Subukia, as soon as I have saved a little more money . . .'

Eunice interrupted. 'Quiet now. That's enough. The band is playing and we may as well show them that we appreciate their efforts.'

Yes, the resident band was playing. There were two couples on the floor. Ali and Wangeci were the third. They looked well matched. Both tall, but Ali just a little taller. And could they dance beautifully? You would have thought that these two had been dancing together since they were kids. Later on in the evening, they asked for something to eat.

They stayed at the 'Three Swallows' for a good three hours. But it was Sunday, not the right day for a late night. So at about ten, they found their way into Ali's black Toyota and disappeared into one of those cheap hotels which are to be found all over the place. They hired a room.

Funny, because they did not go to Ali's flat or house or wherever he lived. Nobody knew where this man lived. Nobody knew who his relatives were. Nobody knew anything about this man apart from what he himself said.

When they got to their hired room, Eunice was the first person to talk.

'Tomorrow is work day, another blue Monday.'

'I am not thinking of tomorrow, Eunice, I am thinking of today.'

'That's typical of you, Ali. You are a today man. What do you say about today, then?'

'Today is Sunday, the day of rest. Would you like to take a little rest?'

'Would I like to take a little rest! Ali, put that question in a more personal way.'

'Well, here it comes. I think you have too many clothes on you.'

'That's what you think.'

'Well, let me find out.'

Eunice Wangeci did not really love this man. He was too careless about life, too unconcerned about his own future. But he had a big title and a good education. Above all, he was a great spender. He could give a girl a nice time. Eunice liked to have a good time with mysterious men. It was something to do with the way she was brought up.

Eunice knew that she was in no danger of being found out by Lewis Maranga. She was certain that he would never find out about her ways. She told herself that she was cleverer than all the men put together. Why should she not please herself the way she wanted while still maintaining her friendship with Lewis?

The following day Lewis was at Ngara at about seven o'clock. He went upstairs and knocked at his girl-friend's door. She was in.

'Eunice, I was here yesterday at about this time, you were not in. I came back at about eight o'clock but you were still not here.'

'I thought I had told you that I would be going to Uthiru. Mummy would not let me come back. Now, I will get you a beer from down below. I will make myself a cup of tea.'

And so it went on. They call it hide and seek. Eunice Wangeci knew all about Lewis Maranga. About his past, about his present, about his imaginary future. The future which they were planning together.

But Lewis Maranga did not know a thing about this girl. He did not have a clue about her past life. He did not have a clue about her present life either. Yet this is the one girl he thought he was in love with. The one girl he was going to marry.

Eunice Wangeci played her cards well. She impressed Lewis Maranga in every way. She did not smoke. She did not drink. She did not do anything else. The perfect girl-friend. The sweetest thing around. Charming, well dressed, well mannered. Lewis was impressed, very impressed. So long as he had that fat bank account, Eunice was going to hang on to him like a tick on a dog's ear. And that is exactly what she did.

Grace Wangare was still looking after the two babies. She was not doing so badly. The Murages now employed a houseboy and this made things a lot easier for Grace. But she was really looking forward to August because Jane Njeri was coming back. She had written to confirm it. Her parents had given her permission to spend the whole of the August holidays at Nairobi. And what could be better than that?

When Jane arrived at last, nobody could stop Grace from talking.

'You look so nice, Jane, so healthy. And you have grown a little taller too. I feel very happy when you are around because I have somebody to talk to. Tell me one thing, Jane, does Lewis write to you?'

Jane swallowed once and then twice. She looked up at the ceiling and said nothing. This was too difficult a question for her to answer.

'All right. You don't want to tell me. But one day I will find out.'

'I am sorry, Grace, but I just cannot get myself to talk about him. But one day I will tell you, no doubt. How are you getting on with Bethwell?'

'We now only talk of marriage. Nothing else.'

'How often have you been there since the time I was here? It is eight months since I was here last, isn't it?'

'Yes, eight months. I go there once or twice a month depending on whether I can get permission. But of course we write to each other quite often.'

'And do you see Lewis Maranga?'

'Sometimes he is in, sometimes he is not.'

'And that girl-friend of his? Her name was Eunice or something.'

'I think they are still together. But I don't know very much about them.'

Jane Njeri went to the bathroom and locked the door. She did not want anybody to see her tears. Those words, 'I think they are still together,' kept ringing in her ears. They were very cruel words.

Bethwell Mbarathi and Lewis Maranga were still living together at Makadara. Often they would sit up late discussing their girls.

'The good thing about Grace is that she takes life naturally. She is very relaxed about things. She has no tensions. She has no psychological complexes. She has a very healthy state of mind.'

'And the trouble with Eunice is that she is too damned strict with herself. She won't do this, she won't do that, she won't do anything.' Lewis was serious.

Bethwell laughs. A kind of derisive, lewd laugh. Maybe he does not have the sort of problems which Lewis Maranga has got.

'Lewis, a girl must be taken as she is. She must be understood in the light of her upbringing. Both Grace and Eunice are good girls in their own ways.'

'Yes, I know. But how much longer can I face this starvation? According to the laws of biology this cannot go on for ever.'

'It can; look at celibate priests.'

'Look at who? Just keep your eyes open, Bethwell. Give me another example. You can forget your priests.'

'Well, people who go to jail. Some of them are locked up for fourteen years.'

'Yes, but they have one or two secrets in those jails. Just talk to somebody who has been there recently.'

'Well, I can't help you much, Lewis. I cannot lend you my Grace. But everything has a cure.'

'Such as?'

'Next door. There is a bar. And some very entertaining bar-maids.'

'And some very entertaining barmaids? Just listen to that. And supposing Eunice came to know about it. Supposing she came to know that I was seen around with a damned barmaid. Believe you me, hell would break loose.'

'Lewis, shall I remind you of the eleventh commandment? Thou shalt not be found out.'

'But I don't think I would really like to associate myself with a barmaid. I care very much for Eunice. She loves me dearly. She thinks of me only. Besides, there is a health factor to consider. Barmaids are indiscriminate. I am very careful of my health, Bethwell.'

'That's nothing. It could be just bad luck. If you end up uncertain of yourself, all you need do is to go to a penicillin bar. But you mustn't mind the syringe. Maybe the last time somebody dropped it nobody bothered to straighten out the needle. But that is a small matter.'

'You still haven't come up with a cure. The cure for starvation, I mean.'

'Promise me three beers and I will tell you of a sure cure.'

'Not the sort of thing that goes on in prisons?'

'No, never. I will show you how to get a live one. With low mileage.'

'A live one and a clean one?'

'Yes. About seventeen, I should think.'

'Bethwell, this is the sweetest thing you have told me for the whole of this year. Make it six beers and not three.'

'Will you throw in a small vodka as well?'

'Yes.'

'And whatever number of soft drinks are required?'

'Yes.'

'Well, Lewis, do you remember last December? The day Grace came here with a very beautiful girl called Jane Njeri?'

'Oh, yes. I do. I remember that girl. We had a few drinks here, we danced, we went up to Ngong Hills. Yes, yes, I remember. That day I was a mug.'

'Well, they are coming here again next Saturday. Don't stare at me as if I were the latest saint to emerge out of the catacombs. Jane Njeri will be here next Saturday. Will you be a mug the second time?'

'No, I assure you I won't. Never again.'

Grace Wangare came up with her tricks as usual. She told Mrs Murage a very long story. But Mrs Murage did not need to hear it all. She knew what her maid wanted. It was all so simple and there was no need to complicate it so much. All that she wanted was a Saturday afternoon off. And of course she wanted to take Jane Njeri with her.

Mrs Murage gave the girls permission to go. She was going to be in and it would not be difficult for her to manage the house. The houseboy would be in too.

Jane Njeri was looking forward very much to this Saturday. All that she wanted in this world was to see Lewis Maranga, to look at him, to talk to him, to hear him talk to her. Above all, she wanted to hear about his feelings. Whether he still remembered her. Whether he ever thought of her. Jane was not very worried about this other girl, Eunice. Young girls in love are never worried about anything. Jane had managed to convince herself that she would marry Lewis one day. She had managed to convince herself that this girl Eunice would disappear into thin air sooner or later.

This time Jane Njeri planned her strategy. She was a lot maturer now, much more of a grown-up girl than she was last December. She told herself that this time she must behave like a good girl. She must make an impression on Lewis Maranga. On no account was she going to give herself away. This was the mistake she made last

December. This was the mistake she must not repeat again. Jane Njeri was very firm on this.

It was a bright Saturday afternoon. Grace Wangare's watch said half past two. A little elegant watch it was. Grace had a light red mini and a very tight black sweater. Jane had the ordinary shoes. But this girl did not need to decorate herself. The eyes, the lips, the hair, all spelled out the word beauty. Natural beauty.

The buses were extremely slow, so it seemed. It took them a whole hour to get to Makadara. But they got there in the long run. The boys were waiting. Lewis Maranga had kept his promise. He had bought a lot of drinks for the occasion. Everybody was ready for everybody else. Especially Lewis Maranga, the starved young man.

Knock, knock, softly and gently. There is movement inside.

'Come in,' somebody says.

The girls moved in. Grace was in the lead. Bethwell was waiting for her with open arms. He swept her from the floor at one go and raised her right up. He is powerfully built. He is also a bit of a ruffian. He held Grace very close and attempted to kiss her. But as soon as their lips touched, Grace turned her neck the other way.

Lewis Maranga had no alternative but to do likewise. Why not? If he did not, it would have looked as if he was the coward in the place. Jane would perhaps have felt unwanted as well. So he swept Jane from her feet and raised her right up. Jane was not as heavy as Grace. But her legs were much longer and her hands were long and fragile. The raising up part was not difficult. But the kissing part did not work because Jane's neck was turned away from Lewis permanently. So Lewis had to make do with kissing the neck itself. Still, that was not bad. In fact, Jane was tickled to death by the experience. She giggled and then laughed loudly.

Once the welcoming ceremony was over the girls were brought back to the vertical position. Everybody sat down. Lewis produced the drinks. Grace cooled herself down with a beer. Bethwell opened one for himself and drank straight out of the bottle. Lewis asked Jane to drink something.

'I will have a soft drink, if you don't mind.'

'A soft drink? Definitely not. The last time you were here you were thriving on better things. Remember?'

'Yes, but today I will take a soda. Fanta, Sprite, Coke, Pepsi, anything like that.'

Jane was adamant and Lewis had no alternative but to offer her a Coke. This girl was going to be difficult. This took Lewis Maranga by surprise because he was not expecting it. He thought it would be plain sailing right from the word go. But the way things were going, it was obvious that Jane was going to be a very difficult nut to crack.

In less than an hour, everybody was high on booze except Jane. She looked miserably sober. A kind of a spoilsport. But she had her plan. She had her intentions. She knew what she wanted. She was not here just to drink and to dance. Not like the last time.

Jane Njeri had already got her reward in part. She had Lewis with her, the boy she so much loved. They were together, if only for what appeared to be a very short time. She also knew that she had impressed him with her determination not to do anything silly. Not to give him the wrong impression of herself. This time was not going to be like the last time.

Before long the record player was put on and music began playing. Jane could not quite make up her mind whether to dance or not to dance. She thought she had better quit dancing altogether. But her inner feelings would not let her. She longed to be in his arms even if this did not mean much. There is a good deal of togetherness in two people dancing. Jane could not bear to forgo this. So she danced with Lewis.

But she was very careful not to allow herself to be held too close by him. Not like the last time. They talked as they danced.

'How is Tumu Tumu? You have only one more term left, haven't you?'

'Yes.'

'And what do you propose to do after that?'

'Get married.'

'Get married? Have you got a boy already lined up?'

'Yes, I have a boy I love. I love him very very much.'

'And who is it?'

Jane Njeri would not answer that question. She just looked up at the ceiling and rolled her eyes from one side to the other. She bit her lips and bit her lips again. She lost one step and then lost two steps.

Lewis Maranga was very smart. He knew that he had touched on a soft point. So he went back to less personal issues.

'Jane, do you remember the day we went on top of the Ngong Hills?'

'Oh, yes, I do.'

'That day you were different.'

'Was I? I wish I had not been. I was too young then. But perhaps we had better not talk about it.'

Lewis Maranga shut up. He looked at Jane from head to foot. She was a good girl in many ways. He was getting quite impressed by her. But perhaps it was too late to be serious. He had to leave that side of things alone and think more about his other intentions. He had some very funny designs on this girl. Maybe he could get from her what he could not get out of Eunice.

Bethwell Mbarathi and Grace Wangare kept talking non-stop as they danced. These two appeared to have a lot to talk about. They had no problems of any kind between them.

It was about five o'clock now and everybody appeared to be tired of dancing. Bethwell took the initiative and introduced the next point on the agenda. He opened the little connecting door, dragged Grace inside, then closed the door again.

Jane and Lewis were now alone. Lewis was in a hurry. It is the way with all men.

'Do you remember the last time you were here, Jane?' he asked.

'Yes, I do, and I was very different from what I am today. I have already told you that.'

'Yes, there is one thing you did not do that time.'

65

'What?'

'On the other side of this curtain there is a bed.'

'Yes, I know.'

'And what are beds made for?'

'For their owners to sleep in.'

Lewis Maranga changed the topic and began talking about Ihithe. About the good old days. About Teacher Andrew Karanja. About the old religious men and women. But deep inside him he was getting afraid, very afraid. It looked as if he would fail in his designs. It looked as if he would have to try any method that would work, fair or foul.

Lewis Maranga knew of only one trick he had not yet used. It is a trick which sometimes works. But if it fails, it can fail miserably. He decided to come out with it.

'Jane, I think of you day and night.' Which was a damned lie.

Jane looked at him in disbelief. Her heart beat fast and her eyes could not see properly.

'Say that again, Lewis.'

'I think of you day and night.'

'I cannot believe you, Lewis. One day you told me that your name was Mark, but this turned out to be all wrong.'

'Well, Jane, I am not telling you about my name now. I am telling you about my feelings.'

Whatever the truth, Jane felt flattered. She told herself that it would be better for Lewis to tell her lies, lots of lies, so long as he talked about love. So long as he talked about both of them.

'Jane, ever since that day way back when I was whipped by Teacher Andrew Karanja because of you,' he continued, 'I have always been thinking about you.'

'And why didn't you tell me so last December?' she asked.

'I thought I better wait for a while. It is no good hurrying up the affairs of the heart.'

'And why didn't you write to me when I went back to Tumu Tumu?'

'I thought of it but I was not quite sure whether this would affect your studies. I mean, I didn't know what would happen if somebody else saw the letter. I mean the headmistress or somebody like that. Don't they read your letters?'

It did not ring true. Jane was not convinced. But still, it was different. She was feeling very good inside. Now she was ready for the final bombshell.

'And what about that girl called Eunice?' she asked.

Lewis was not expecting this question. He had no ready answer. He had no time to think either. So he said whatever came into his head.

'Eunice? Who told you about her? We have already broken up. That girl pretends to be very good but she is not. I would not be surprised if she goes about with other men. Nairobi is full of crooks and I suspect that Eunice goes about with some of these crooks.'

Lewis was winning the battle. He was getting somewhere at long last. He knew this because he could see Jane's eyes getting a little wet.

'Lewis, how can you prove to me that what you are saying is true?'

'This way.'

Lewis got hold of Jane's hands and wrapped himself up with them. He then gave her a long passionate kiss.

Jane Njeri melted like butter on a hot stove. Lewis Maranga now played with her as if she was made of plasticine. Within minutes she was on the bed, listening to more phoney stories. Stories of fake love. How they will get married one day. How they will raise a family. And such other rubbish. For the whole night.

The girls went back to Kilimani Estate the following morning. After they had left, Bethwell looked at Lewis and asked, 'Lewis, is Jane Njeri still a virgin?'

Lewis Maranga paused for a while then said, 'Yes, she was. Yesterday evening.'

4

The last term at Tumu Tumu was hectic. Jane Njeri knew that she had to work hard to pass. She had to forget everything else, apart from Lewis Maranga, of course. He was unforgettable.

She often talked about Lewis Maranga to the other girls. The other girls talked about their boy-friends too. This is what girls do at school after classes. This is what they do when they go to their dormitories to sleep. Jane used to talk to Mary Wambui often. Mary Wambui had been her friend for a long time. Besides, it would soon be the end of the last term.

'Mary, I know that your Joseph must be waiting for you. We'll be out of this place soon, don't forget.'

'Yes, he will be waiting for me with open arms. I think this time I will allow him to kiss me for the first time.'

'What does Joseph do? Might he be a carpenter, by any chance?'

'No, Jane. But he almost became a carpenter at one time. He tells me that he is a mason, a kind of a building engineer. Is your Lewis a carpenter, by any chance?'

'No, Mary. My Lewis works with a beer company. Is your Joseph romantic?'

'No, he appears to be afraid of me. But I like it that way. And what about Lewis?'

'Lewis is a problem from head to foot.'

'You are lucky, Jane. At times I think that a romantic boy is better than a dormant one like my Joseph.'

Jane laughed because she understood. She was a big girl now. Big enough to be able to postpone problems. She knew she had a problem herself that she would not think about it until after the final examinations. Until she was out of Tumu Tumu for good. Until she was back at Ihithe where the wind blows gently and the evenings are cool and serene. Yes, Jane had a problem which she did not want to think about.

For the whole of the last term at school, Jane Njeri was living in an unreal world suspended somewhere between the probable and the possible. Her mental faculties were in a permanent state of near collapse. But she refused to collapse because she refused to think. She refused to think about the stoppage of her monthly habit, the habit of all healthy mature girls. She completely refused to meditate on her possible pregnancy.

Jane Njeri was not an experienced girl because of the way she had been brought up, but she had a stout heart. She had the will of a matador and the energy of a bulldozer. She knew of her problem and she knew what the problem was. She even knew where she had collected the problem from. How could she forget? How could she forget the night Lewis said he loved her?

The final examination papers were not too difficult. Jane was sure she did well in her School Certificate examination. She was glad to turn her back on Tumu Tumu for the last time.

She thought about her problem once she was out of Tumu Tumu. There was a lot of time for weeping alone quietly. There was a lot of time for self-pity, for remorse, for bafflement, for utter disappointment.

Jane Njeri often wondered why it had to happen to her. Why not to any of the other girls at Tumu Tumu? Why at this time of her life? Why should this happen to the only child in the family, the only daughter? Why to the daughter of a church minister?

If Bwana Absalom came to know about it, he would go raving mad. He would skin her alive. He would hang her on the nearest tree. He would not bury her with the other Christians. Christians do not get pregnant before they are married. They do not get pregnant after such an upright upbringing. Only heathens do it. Only the children of pagans do it. Jane Njeri knew her father well. On no account must he come to know.

But Jane Njeri was not quite so sure about how her mother Agatha would react to the sad news. Would she throw herself into a fury? Would she break all the pots and smash all the pans? Would she tear her clothes in anger or set Jane's bedroom alight? No, not quite. Mother Agatha was not that type. She was just not moulded that way. Above all, there was that tender motherly love between mother and daughter. The only daughter. Jane Njeri was ready to try, to risk, to expose, to talk. If Agatha would not listen, nobody else would.

Jane Njeri chose a good moment. It was in the morning when mother and daughter were sipping a cup of mid-morning tea. Bwana Absalom was out at the church doing his own Christian things.

'Mummy, I would like to go to Nairobi to stay with the Murages.'

'Why? They have got a houseboy now and I do not think that they need extra help.'

'It is not because of that, mummy. I need some medical attention.'

'Medical attention? You look healthy all over. What is the matter with you, Jane? You are not sick, are you?'

'It is my kidneys, mummy. There must be something wrong with my kidneys. This trouble appears to have triggered off high blood-pressure. I am certain I have high blood-pressure. I am often afflicted by persistent headaches. Or it could be migraine? I must see a physician. Gideon knows many doctors who can help me.'

Jane did not tell the truth. She had faltered at the last moment. Maybe just as well, because she had saved Agatha a lot of disappointment. Whatever her reaction would have been, Agatha would definitely not have been happy to hear that her daughter was looking forward to being a mother, an unmarried mother.

Agatha discussed her daughter's health with Bwana Absalom. They agreed that their daughter was not looking too well of late and that she required expert medical attention. Besides, she might be able to get a vacation job at Nairobi. If she could earn herself a little money, this would not do her any harm at all.

'And remember, Agatha,' Absalom told his wife, 'our daughter is now a big girl. She can definitely look after herself now. Her straight upbringing is bound to help her tremendously when she goes out into life.'

'Precisely, Absalom.' Agatha is very obliging.

'But I have one fear, Agatha. Girls change when they finish school. They feel free.'

'What is your fear?' Agatha asked.

'This freedom is not a good thing. A lot of girls have found themselves in a lot of trouble because of doing foolish things with boys. A rocky foundation can be ruined by a small stupid thing.'

'Jane Njeri would never do a thing like that. We have been careful with her. She knows what to do and what not to do in life.'

'But I will have a few words with her, just to make sure,' Bwana Absalom concluded.

The few words were said on the evening before Jane Njeri left Ihithe for Nairobi. These were words of wisdom. Only wisdom passes from the mouth of Bwana Absalom Gacara to the little beautiful head of his only daughter who rejoices in the name of Jane Njeri.

'Jane, tomorrow you will go to Nairobi. Greet your uncle Gideon very warmly, together with all his family.'

'I will do that, papa.'

'Tell him to look round just in case he can get you a job to do. You can now earn yourself a little money.'

'I will do that, papa.'

'Be careful in Nairobi. That place is full of temptations. You will be tempted to do a lot of unchristian things which could ruin your life. Keep away from all these temptations.'

'I will do that, papa.'

'Boys, especially. You can do a little stupid thing which could ruin the whole of your life. Being pregnant before marriage, for example. This could change your whole life. It might mean having to stay without a job. It might mean that you might never get married the whole of your life. It would be a great shame to your parents. Be careful that you do not do anything silly with a boy.'

'I will be careful, papa.'

'Do you understand what I mean by doing a silly thing with a boy?'

'Yes, papa, I understand.'

Jane Njeri understood. She was a big girl now in the literal sense of the word. What she longed for was an escape from the world of Ihithe, the world that was hostile and intolerable. She needed a companion, like Grace Wangare. She needed a liberated home, like Gideon's. Above all, she wanted to talk to Lewis Maranga.

Grace Wangare was very happy to see Jane Njeri back. The Murages were delighted to hear the latest news from Ihithe. Jane had always been very willing to help in the house and this made her very welcome at the Murages' home where there was always a lot of work to do.

Before long, the girls were talking. Grace Wangare is an observant girl and she had already noted a change in Jane.

'Jane, you must be putting on weight,' she said.

'I have no worries, that's why.'

Jane had definitely tried desperately to hide her four months' pregnancy. Only a trained eye could notice one or two suspicious symptoms here and there.

'You are so lucky to finish school without a mishap, Jane. Many girls these days simply cannot finish their studies properly. Boys do not give them any peace. Sometimes it is their teachers. Sometimes it is other people. These days even ordinary girls like ourselves have to be careful. With a boy like Bethwell Mbarathi, I myself have to be vary careful, you know. All normal boys are madmen, I tell you . . .'

'Quiet a bit, Grace. How do you be careful if you have a boy who is difficult to handle?'

'Is Lewis Maranga difficult? Do you mean to tell me that he has been coming all the way to Tumu Tumu at night?'

'Answer my question, Grace. The one about how to be careful.'

'I will tell you some other time. It is not necessary now, not until we go to Makadara. Then it may be necessary. I wonder why you have never asked me this question before. What else do you want to know from me?'

'How to contact Lewis Maranga today. It must be today, Grace.'

'Today? Why all the hurry?'

'You don't understand everything, Grace. But is it possible to contact Lewis today?'

It was urgent. Grace Wangare is no fool and never was one. She snatched a moment when the children were asleep and took Jane to the shops. There was a public call-box there. Grace would never use the home telephone without permission.

'Is that Kenya Beer Agencies?'

'Yes. Can I help you?'

'Can I speak to Mr Lewis Maranga, please?'

'Hold on.'

Jane Njeri now took the phone. It was her first time to speak into this thing.

'Can I speak to Mr Lewis Maranga?' she said.

'Speaking.'

'Hello, who is speaking?'

'Lewis Maranga here. Can I help you?'

'Yes. Because I am expecting your baby.'

Bang and out. Lewis was not going to listen. Jane Njeri was now shedding her usual quiet tears. Grace Wangare was now in a state of shock because she understood why Jane Njeri appeared to have been putting on weight. But she was bold enough to call Lewis Maranga on the line again.

'This is Grace Wangare. Remember?'

'Yes. And who was talking to me before?'

'The beautiful tall girl from Ihithe. Remember? The one you

got beaten up for by Teacher Andrew Karanja. Remember?'

'Yes, I remember, so what?'

'She is distressed. She is crying. Remember what she has just told you?'

'Yes. I remember. But tell her to think of another boy. Tell her she has guessed it all wrong. Tell her that I am getting married to Eunice next August and she can go and jump into the lake because I cannot start off with two wives. And please, Grace, do tell this girl not to mix up her boy-friends like that.'

There were two very sad people in that call-box that morning. Two shattered girls. But they were very kind to each other. They walked back home quietly, holding hands.

Mrs Murage is a trained hospital nurse. She has the eyes of an eagle when it comes to telling what is normal and what is not normal. That is her job and that is what she is paid for. She had already noted one or two changes in Jane.

'Gideon, this girl Jane Njeri. I think she is pregnant.'

'You do, do you? I thought that was what girls are made for. Or it could be the good food you give her.'

'I am certain of it and I am not surprised. Jane is not the type that boys would run away from, you know. We must do something about it fairly soon.'

'Otherwise?' Gideon asked.

'We'll soon have three babies in the house.'

'If she doesn't have twins, that is. Talk to her one of these fine days. She will no doubt find it easier to tell you her secrets than me. Take her to a place in town and tell her all about boys and girls. Jane is probably quite ignorant about boys. Don't forget she is the daughter of a church minister.'

Mrs Murage knew that she had a difficult job to do. Talking to a girl who has just left school and who is suspected of being pregnant is not an easy matter. Should it be that she is actually pregnant, it would be even more difficult to know what to do to help her. But Mrs Murage had helped many people in trouble. She knew how to deal with difficult problems of this nature.

Mrs Murage chose a good day. It was Sunday, late in the afternoon. Jane Njeri had never been at the Nairobi City Park before. That's where they went. What she saw there were trees and nothing but trees, but it was cool and peaceful. Mrs Murage talked a lot about trees and forests. How forests attract rain and provide wood. How parks keep the towns beautiful. How important it is to have fresh air and so on and so forth. It all sounded very dull to Jane. She had heard it all at school.

Jane Njeri thought of mentioning her problem to Mrs Murage. She knew that the Murages had noted that she was no longer what she used to be. She really wanted to discuss her pregnancy with Mrs Murage. Perhaps there was something that could be done even at this late stage. Perhaps there was somebody who could be of use. After all, this was not the first time that a girl had got pregnant. It was not the last time either. But if this talk about trees and flowers went on the way it was going, Jane Njeri would go back home a disappointed girl.

Mrs Murage now suggested that they should go back to the car. Jane Njeri's fears came true. They were going back home without saying anything of use. What a pity.

But no. Mrs Murage went towards the town. She said that she knew of a quiet place somewhere along Kimathi Street. They would go there for a coffee or a cold drink and then go back home. They headed straight for the 'Three Swallows', this new place with a sliding door. The place that looks rather dark inside.

Yes, it was not very bright inside at all. But there were quite a lot of people there. They were mainly couples or little groups of people. Mrs Murage pointed to a little table for two. They went and sat there. From there, they could see most of the people who were inside. They had a good view of the dancing floor in front of them. There were musical instruments in one corner. They play music in this place. Nobody could have chosen a better place than the 'Three Swallows'.

Someone came to serve them and Mrs Murage ordered two Martinis. It was half past six, time for a little quiet drink.

'Have you ever tasted Martini before, Jane?'

'No. I wish you had not ordered one for me. Is it a strong drink?'

'No, it is a sweet drink. You will like it. What would you have chosen?'

'I really don't know. My daddy always says that a girl should take coffee, or milk, or soda.'

'Jane, you are a grown-up girl now. Do you still stick to what mummy and daddy told you when you were a baby?'

'No, not quite. But they have influenced my life quite a lot.'

'My parents were much the same as yours, Jane. But I became a rebel at the age of fifteen. So much of what they told me was utter old-fashioned nonsense.'

Jane laughed. She liked that part. She had considered herself a rebel ever since the day she tasted beer for the first time out there at Makadara.

The Martini was nice and sweet. She liked it. But it tasted rather strong to her. It was making her gullet and stomach warm.

Mrs Murage now opened her handbag. Jane thought that she was looking for money to pay for the drinks. Once again, Jane feared that they would be packing up for home without having said a word about anything of value. But she was not to be disappointed.

Mrs Murage pulled out what looked like a fair-sized brown card. She handed this thing to Jane. It had a lot of white tablets stuck to it by some transparent material. Next to each table was written a date.

'Guess what that is?'

'Not a clue. Or . . . wait. Some kind of medicine?'

'Yes and no. These are called contraceptive pills. They stop women from getting pregnant if they do not want to.'

Jane Njeri became extremely interested in these white tablets. She had always thought that if there was anything that could stop women from getting pregnant if they didn't want to, it was men.

That is as far as she had gone. Now, if white tablets could do the trick, this world must be full of surprises.

But she had to be careful not to look too interested. Deep inside her she was feeling remorseful because pills would not be of much use to her now.

'How are these used? How does one get them?' she asked.

Mrs Murage explained how they are used, in a simple straightforward manner. She also explained how one gets them.

'On top of all that, Jane,' she said, 'they are free.'

Jane could not understand why Mrs Murage had failed so miserably in spacing her own children. Not with all these pills around. Two babies in fifteen months cannot be called good spacing.

'Mrs Murage, do these things really work? I mean, are they reliable?' she asked.

'Yes, provided you don't forget to swallow the thing. But if you forget, you cannot blame the pill, can you?'

Mrs Murage talked about other methods. About devices and protectives. About the work being done to come up with better and safer methods. She even talked about the safe periods. Jane was listening very attentively.

Jane liked the Martini but it was now getting quite low. Mrs Murage ordered another round but this time she asked for a beer for herself.

'I will change to beer myself but you better keep to Martini. I always start off with something sweet but then the sweetness overcomes me.'

Jane Njeri wanted to comment on the bitterness of beer but she did not want Mrs Murage to know that she had tasted beer before.

The atmosphere was now quite relaxed. It was also getting rather dark outside. More and more people were pouring into the 'Three Swallows'. Five uniformed gentlemen were now examining the musical instruments. The band would be playing before long, no doubt. They play music here, even on Sundays.

'Thank you very much for explaining all these things to me, Mrs

Murage. It is the first time it has been explained to me so clearly. I have read a certain amount of it in books, but books do not make things clear sometimes.'

'I am glad to know that I have been of some use to you, Jane.'

'But then, Mrs Murage, there is one thing that the books never talk about.'

Jane hesitated. She looked around to see whether anybody was listening. There was one couple directly behind her. A tall handsome boy with a very smooth dark skin. The girl also had dark features. She looked fairly tall. She wore a wig, a very tight sweater and a miniskirt. But they did not appear to be listening. They were drinking beer, and talking quite a lot. They looked quite intimate, these two.

'Mrs Murage, why don't books say what one should do if those methods which you told me about don't work? What do you do if they fail completely?'

'You mean if those methods fail and one gets pregnant?'

'Yes, and you are not married?'

Mrs Murage's moment of truth had come. She had wanted to introduce this topic later on in the evening, but her delaying tactics had obviously failed. It all pointed to the urgency of the situation.

'Jane, let us get more personal,' she said.

'Yes, indeed. You know everything. You know my problem. You can see it. You are a hospital nurse. I need your help, Mrs Murage.'

It was out of her lungs at long last. She was very relieved now that she had said it as it should be said. Yet, it was not as difficult as she thought it would be. Not at all difficult with a broad-minded person like Mrs Murage.

'Jane, let us start from the bottom.'

'Yes. Where?'

'Is the boy interested in you?'

'We can forget him.'

'According to tradition, we can make him pay for the support of the child.'

'You are going too fast, Mrs Murage. There are only four people who know about this. The boy, Grace, you and me. I don't want anybody else to know about it if we can help it. Let us keep tradition out of all this. It would bring in parents. I don't want my parents to know. I hate to imagine what they would do to me if they came to know.'

'Let me think. This is a difficult problem.' Mrs Murage bit her lip.

'Mrs Murage, haven't you people got tablets or something that one can take?'

'Jane, abortion is illegal. How long is it since . . .'

'Four months.'

'At four months it could even be fatal. Forget about it. There is a legal way out of every problem.'

Now they were talking. The drinks were helping them to talk. The great barrier of secrecy between them had been broken.

The band now began playing. Almost everybody looked in front and stopped talking. The sound was good. Some eager souls even began tapping the floor gently with their feet. But not the boy and the girl behind. These ones woke up immediately, strode out to the floor and began dancing. They danced nicely as if they had been dancing together since they were kids. Before long, other couples joined them.

'Life is funny, Jane. Do you see that couple dancing out there? The tall dark boy and the girl with a tight sweater? Maybe they think that one day they will get married.'

'Could be. Why not?'

'Because one marries someone very different from what one might suppose originally. Somebody one never imagined. A boy comes right from the blues, you fall in love with him and he marries you before you know what you are doing.'

'How do you explain that, Mrs Murage?'

'I can't explain it. It is one of the interesting things in this world. I guess if I were a religious person I would call it a mystery.'

'You mean I may end up marrying somebody I do not know?'

'Precisely. I had a steady boy-friend myself for seven years. Seven years is not a short time, Jane. We were deeply in love. Honey sweet, mellow love, like the fragrance of a rose.'

'Then what happened?'

'We had a few small problems here and there but I decided to ignore them completely. But my boy did not. He kept talking about them. I think I was growing more mature than he was. Before long we were out of step with each other.'

'And then?'

'We had a little stupid quarrel one day and he wrote a letter to me saying that I did not love him and that he could do without me. That was the end. I could no longer stand a boy who was behaving like a little child.'

'Oh, what a pity.'

'For three years I refused to have anything to do with boys. I avoided their company completely. It was then that I realised how foolish teenage love can be.'

'Do you call it foolish?'

'Then, out of nowhere comes Gideon. He captures my imagination. He talks about life in a reasonable way. He has firm ideas about love, job, family, money, religion. He impresses me as a man who knows where he comes from and where he is going. So different from that childish boy-friend of mine. We are in love and within nine months we are married. This is how mature love comes. It falls on you like a ton of bricks. But you are nevertheless able to keep your head. You are able to think and to be reasonable.'

'Yet you must admit, Mrs Murage, that first love is very very strong.'

'Oh yes, Jane, nothing can be stronger than that. You cannot sleep. You cannot think about anything else but him. Your whole life gets wrapped up in this boy. You read his letters ten times. You look at his picture fifteen times in one morning. You do all sorts of other stupid things.'

'Do you call them stupid, Mrs Murage?'

Jane Njeri was listening very carefully. Her love for Lewis Maranga was definitely unreasonable. It was definitely unproductive. Yet deep in her heart she had not yet given him up. Not yet.

'Mrs Murage, what you say is very true. Many girls have gone through this love experience without thinking.'

'Jane, if you can reason, then it is not your first love. If you have been in love with a boy for seven years, then you better give him up. You will never marry him.'

The music stopped and the dancing partners came back to their seats. The couple who were sitting behind them came back holding hands. The girl sat down. The tall boy said something.

'Thanks very much, Eunice. That was a lovely dance,' he said.

'Thanks, Ali. Today they are playing better than they were playing yesterday.'

Jane Njeri virtually jumped out of her skin. She almost fainted with confusion. Eunice? Or was it a coincidence? Could it be possible? How could she find out? She came up with a solution.

'Mrs Murage,' she said, 'I love a boy called Lewis Maranga.' Jane said this very loudly. They heard it all the way to the counter where they were dishing out drinks. They heard it all the way to the band. And of course Ali and Eunice heard it only too well.

Eunice Wangeci looked back instantly. Jane Njeri looked back as well. Their eyes met for one fleeting moment. Then they both looked back towards their tables in a hurry. Jane had achieved her purpose. This girl could have been no other person other than Eunice Wangeci. But the boy was not Lewis Maranga. That was for sure.

'Jane, please don't be so loud,' Mrs Murage said. 'Or maybe the Martini is doing its work?' Mrs Murage was certainly worried about Jane's rather loud confession. But she was not aware of the drama that was going on around her.

Eunice Wangeci said something to Ali Kamau and they both rose to leave. Jane Njeri now looked at them unashamedly. Ali stared at her as if she was the daughter of a zebra.

'Mrs Murage, don't you think that we had better go home?'

'Are you happy now?'

'No. I am extremely unhappy.'

'Why?'

'Because I have still got my problem with me. I still do not know what to do. I do not know where I am heading for. Is there no way out of this predicament?'

'There must be. I have a few hazy ideas about one or two possible solutions, but I must speak to my husband first. Gideon knows a lot of people and a lot of places. He is useful at a time like this. That is what a good husband should be. I will let you know what we decide.'

That was the end of the evening, and what an evening it was. When they got back home, Jane began thinking. She was a lot wiser now. About methods, for example. About Eunice Wangeci. About unproductive love.

Young love does not die easily. Neither did Jane's. She was prepared to give it one more chance, just one more. The chance came in the shape of a letter she wrote to Lewis Maranga. A love-letter, no doubt, but with a difference. She talked of having met Eunice Wangeci with a tall dark boy called Ali. They were both drinking beer. They were both dancing. They were holding hands. She wrote freely and without undue emotion. She was learning to be reasonable. Above all, she wanted to be truthful.

Was Maranga going to be reasonable? No. His answer was simple and straightforward. He was not going to listen to any lies. Eunice Wangeci would never do such a thing. It might have been somebody else. Her elder sister, for example. Her distant cousin, perhaps. Lewis Maranga ended his letter on a rather nasty note. He said that he was not much interested in receiving letters from a girl with a sick head.

That was the end of the road as far as Jane Njeri was concerned. What Mrs Murage had told her had strengthened her heart considerably. She could now forget Lewis Maranga without any regrets. She had no bitterness in her heart whatsoever. She was now convinced that her love for him was an essential process in growing up, no more. Jane Njeri was growing up, that was all.

Memories of Lewis Maranga disappeared into thin air within weeks. But it was now obvious to everybody that Jane Njeri was expecting a baby. The Murages promised her that they would not reveal her pregnancy to her parents. This was very good news. They also said that they were going ahead with arrangements to have the child adopted immediately after birth. This was their plan and Jane Njeri was ready to accept it.

But not without a good deal of bitterness in her heart. She would have liked to see her baby, at least for some time. She would have liked to show Lewis Maranga this baby one day in the future. What father would not be interested in his own baby?

A letter came announcing the good news that Jane Njeri had obtained a first-grade pass in her School Certificate examination. She was third in her glass. She had been admitted for the Advanced Certificate at the Alliance Girls' High School.

If this letter was not answered, there might be inquiries about her. She wrote back immediately and said that she would not be available. She had to forget about further education. From now on, she was going to think in terms of what was reasonable, feasible, practicable. Her first worry would be this pregnancy of hers. After that, she could concentrate on other things.

Weeks rolled by. Jane worked in the house to the best of her ability. Mrs Murage occasionally took her to the obstetric wing of the Kenyatta National Hospital for examination. It had been agreed between Mrs Murage and her husband that they would not reveal the details of their plan to Jane. They had succeeded in gaining her full confidence and this is what mattered more than anything else.

And Grace Wangare? She was a great source of comfort to Jane Njeri. Above all, she confirmed that the methods which Mrs Murage talked about work. It was strange that a girl like Grace Wangare should have known what Jane Njeri had never heard about. This is a strange world.

Grace was optimistic that everything would end up all right. Her trips to Makadara were now less frequent. She did not see Lewis Maranga on the few occasions when she went there. Anyhow, all this was rather unimportant now because Jane was not interested in Lewis any more.

May is a rainy month in Nairobi. Long ago, April used to be the rainy month, but it no longer is. I guess that old people will tell you that long, long ago, it was March that used to be the rainy month. The world moves round in circles and everything seems to be changing, including the weather. The world is drying up, that's for sure.

In May, Kilimani Estate is a beautiful place. The grass is green and the flower gardens are colourful. When it rains, the children go out in the rain exactly as they used to do in the olden days. They believe that rain will make them grow tall. But they make sure that their mothers do not see them doing this. The old ladies would catch pneumonia.

When the time came, Jane Njeri was sad to say farewell to Kilimani Estate. She was sad to say farewell to Grace Wangare and the Murage family. She did not know where Mrs Murage was taking her to. But she could guess. She was being taken to an institution which looks after unwed mothers. There, she would have her child but she would never see it. It would be taken away immediately for adoption. She had agreed to this plan and she had signed all the necessary papers.

Mrs Murage knew her way through Nairobi. At times Jane Njeri did not know where they were or where they were heading for. But it was not long before they came to an area she knew. Makadara. She forced herself to look the other way so as not to see the housing block where her former boy-friend probably still lived.

It was a quiet journey all the way to the Smiles Mothers' Home. The big gate was opened for them and they drove straight to the main building which contained the office.

As soon as they stepped out of the car, Jane Njeri felt a cold shudder go through her spine. This was going to be her home for the next few days. She would be together with a number of other girls who had failed in life like her. Ignorant, stupid, pregnant girls. Girls who had brought shame to themselves and their parents. Girls who now required pity and help because they had committed one of the most grievous crimes on record.

But Jane Njeri was ready for it all. Somehow, this girl was now ready to face anything. Even this. She even managed to smile as they entered the office of the Mother Superior. She was there, waiting for them. Somebody brought coffee as soon as they were seated.

Jane Njeri looked at the Mother Superior. She looked at the white robes, the headgear, the oversize crucifix on the chest. She gazed at the religious pictures on the wall. They reminded her of her young days. They reminded her of her old Bible in pictures. But these ones were very big. They almost looked real.

The formalities did not take long. Before long, Mrs Murage was saying good-bye.

'I will be back within a few days. The Sisters here will look after you. They are very kind. So do not worry, Jane. You are a young girl and you have a lot of time ahead of you.'

Jane nodded her head. She bit her lip as she saw Mrs Murage go. Sister Angela showed her to her room. Sister Angela was a black Sister. She looked very cheerful. She showed Jane where the dining-room was, the church, the rest-room, everything. She introduced her to some of the inmates. They were mostly young girls, good-looking girls. They all had one thing in common. They were not victims of sterility or childlessness. Not a bad thing, if you look at it that way.

When Sister Angela left, Jane rested in her room for a while and then went to the bathroom. There is nothing in this world that can surpass a good hot bath inside one of those large bathtubs that they have at the Smiles Mothers' Home. Taking a bath is a wonderful thing because it is one of the few moments in life when you have a chance to see yourself exactly as you are. It is the only time in life when your eyes can look at the truth, the naked truth. For Jane, it was the protruding truth, the rounded truth, the tender truth.

Jane Njeri had never been in a Catholic institution before. She was free to say prayers in her own way but she took this opportunity to learn how to make the sign of the cross and to say prayers on her knees with her eyes wide open. It took some time because at Ihithe people say their prayers while seated and with their eyes closed and covered with the hands.

The Sisters were very kind. Their minds were clean and the kindness that came from their hearts was as pure as the fragrance of a jasmine flower. She had never seen dedication carried to this degree. She had never seen devotion to duty carried to these heights. The Sisters instilled a new life into her. Above all, nobody called her a sinner or a stupid, immoral bitch. In this institution, human dignity mattered before all else.

Even the doctor was a Sister. She was only called in when required. The Mother Superior together with Sister Angela could deal with minor problems but not with the actual delivery.

The girls in this institution were all very friendly. They had to be. Friendliness often comes out of sharing a common knock. All the girls here had been knocked. They all had a knock in the engine, so to speak. And did they tell their stories? They did, often amid loud, artificial laughter. Just listen to them.

'This boy told me that he loved me. I was in love with him myself. He told me that we would get married and have children. And so we started having children there and then. But then, when I told him about my condition, he came up with the suggestion that I should start off the family without him. He promised to join me later. He hasn't come round to joining me yet. And I don't think he is ever coming.'

'My boy was different. He told me that he would do nothing of the kind. But he kept complaining that his bed was too big for him. One day he managed to get me inside that bed. He promised not to touch me. So he faced that way and I faced the other way. But I am a very sleepy type. I snore the whole night through. I still don't know what he did but I know the results.'

'Mine was different. He was a great coward. He was afraid of me. But I loved him. Everybody else talked to me about their boys. They told me how they were having great fun doing all sorts of things. So I made up my mind that I couldn't continue being the odd girl out, the only girl with no story to tell. One day something happened. It was at a party. He became very romantic. He pulled me to the garden behind the house. I did not feel like refusing. But this boy was useless. Such a big boy but he did not appear to know a thing. I taught him how. One could say that I brought this problem on myself. And see where it has got me.'

At long last, Jane Njeri's time came. It all began in the evening. The doctor was called. Jane was transferred to the delivery wing. She had a baby at five o'clock in the morning of May 15th. But she never saw the baby.

In six days' time, Jane Njeri was ready to go back home. Mrs Murage came for her. Tearful good-byes were said. It was a happy day but full of sadness.

Back at Kilimani Estate, Jane Njeri was now a new girl. Straight, upright and chastised. Sweet, smooth but full of uncertainties. Always thinking about that baby. What was its sex? What did it look like? Where was the child now?

Gideon Murage was a good man when it came to solving problems. This time the problem was simple and straightforward. A single girl with a first-class School Certificate wanted a job. Any job, clerical or otherwise. Gideon Murage contacted the people he knew. Jane Njeri was offered a job at a bank. This is a good bank because it also employs people like Eunice Wangeci, Ali Kamau, Thuo Thenge, and a lot of other people. She was to report on July 1st.

On July 1st, this bank on Government Road took on a new employee in the shape of a minister's daughter. A tall beautiful girl called Jane Njeri.

5

People who work in banks are very busy all the time. But they were not too busy to note the arrival of this new girl who was now working downstairs. The boys talked about Jane Njeri during coffee time. They stared at her when she came into the office in the morning and stared at her when she left in the evening. But boys tend to fear very beautiful girls. They just look at them and leave them alone.

But there was one bachelor in this bank who did not fear beautiful girls. Ali Kamau was the adventurous type of bachelor, the type that likes teasing girls and pinching their bottoms. Ali Kamau now began dreaming about Jane Njeri. He wanted to make friends with this girl. He had a hundred and one reasons why he would have wanted to take this girl into his confidence.

One reason was that he was through with Eunice Wangeci. Their friendship had fizzled out somehow and they were no longer going out together at week-ends. Ali Kamau had already got what he wanted from Eunice. Don't get me wrong, because Ali Kamau is the sort of man who wants all sorts of things from young girls. Now that he was absolutely fed up with Eunice Wangeci, he wanted somebody else for a change. Somebody to take to the 'Three Swallows' at week-ends.

Eunice Wangeci was a little disappointed that Ali Kamau was slowly getting her out of the way. Perhaps it was her fault because she made herself too easily available to him. But she did not really feel the loss, if it could be called a loss. Her boy Lewis Maranga was there. They were going to get married that very August. Eunice forgot Ali Kamau once and for all.

Her only regret was that she had found out so little about this man. She did not know where he lived, or what his background was. All she knew was that he worked in the same bank with her, no more. She was not even certain that he was a bachelor. Maybe he had a wife in another town somewhere, who knows? Ali Kamau was a complete mystery to her.

At about this time, Eunice Wangeci came to know why her boy friend Lewis Maranga had such a fat account in the bank. She found this out in a very interesting way. Lewis asked her to do something for him in conjunction with the records clerk, Thuo Thenge. At first Eunice was reluctant to do it because it was all so strange. It was also a very dangerous operation. On top of that, it was illegal. But it sounded exciting, very exciting indeed. And the result? The fat account became even fatter. Nobody found out. All was well.

Eunice liked this account. It was the bond that joined her to Lewis. It was what had made her find out about Lewis Maranga in the first place. Money is good. A girl like Eunice who grew up near Nairobi knows that money is good. Eunice Wangeci is not Jane Njeri.

Three months after she had worked with the bank, not many people would have recognised Absalom's daughter. She wore the most gorgeous clothes and decorated herself in a very alluring manner. She was no longer living with the Murages now. She had managed to rent herself a one-room flat on the top floor of a commercial building along Latema Road. This was very convenient because her bank was just round the corner and she did not need to bother about buses. Bus fares can add up to quite a lot of money.

Jane Njeri's body and mind were undergoing a tremendous change. The body was straight once more. The fair, fragile features were now even more noticeable than before. There was some money around, although not very much, and Jane knew how to use it to project her new image. A girl like this did not need to try all that hard. But Jane was not going to leave anything to chance. Not her. She was going to be careful. Mrs Murage's advice had to be put into practice. How?

One Wednesday afternoon, she hid herself from work and went to a family planning clinic. She had heard about a device that is fitted by doctors. Many girls were very enthusiastic about this thing. She wanted to find out what it was all about. At the clinic she gave her name as Mary Thama. The doctor at the clinic was very helpful. Above all, he appeared to be rather talkative.

'With this you do not need any pills,' he said.

'Yeah? But I will take them all the same, Doctor.'

'I strongly advise you against it. Use one or the other method, but not both.'

'Yeah? But if you knew what I have gone through, you wouldn't say that.'

Dr Donald Kalule was about thirty. He did not look married. He had not met such a stubborn girl for a long, long time. Stubborn but stunningly beautiful.

'If you are intending to use pills on top of this, you'd better let me know so that I may stop doing what I am doing.'

'What's your advice? This one or the pills?'

'There are some disadvantages connected with both of them.'

'Such as?'

'Pills have been alleged to interfere with blood pressure.'

'Then I'll cut them out. What does this one interfere with?'

'Nothing. Unless your boy-friend is very tall. The tall ones sometimes complain.'

'That's the method I want. I have no boy-friend and nobody will complain.'

Dr Kalule was a little puzzled. 'Then what's the point of going through all this if you have no boy-friend?'

'Rapes are on the increase, Doctor. I thought you knew.'

Dr Kalule shook his head. He was really wondering whether he should not have a few words with this girl one day in his office. He felt he had a duty to put her mind right on family planning. She had a lot of wrong ideas about contraception.

'That's that. It is fitted,' he said. 'But I would like to talk to you about family planning some time when I am not holding a clinic. Would you be interested?'

'Yes. Give me the day and the time.'

'Any day apart from Wednesdays. But you must make an appointment.'

'What's your phone number, Doctor?' Dr Kalule gave her a card.

Jane looked at the card. Then she read it aloud. 'Doctor Donald Kalule, Consultant in . . . what's this long word?'

'Obstetrics.'

'And what is the other long word?'

'Gynaecology.'

'Holy Lord. And what do they all mean?'

Dr Kalule virtually ordered Jane out of the room. Good-looking girls have always been a problem. Doctors are human beings, you know. Dr Kalule did not want to see Jane go so soon. But he could not detain her any longer. There was a long queue of young girls all waiting to be attended to. But not to worry. She was going to come back one of these fine days. There was that little lecture about family planning which she had said that she would like to listen to.

Jane Njeri was now a different person altogether. Her mind, especially, had undergone a tremendous change. She was no longer the inward-looking girl she used to be. Jane was now totally liberated. Her mind was open about everything, perhaps a bit too open. She was now a modern girl, perhaps a little too modern. Beautiful, tough and completely self-reliant, that was Jane.

Within a few days Jane was on the phone. She knew the number.

'Dr Kalule, please.'

'Speaking.'

'It's Mary Thama here. Do you remember me?'

'Oh, yes. I will give you an appointment for Tuesday, two o'clock.'

'Dr Kalule, don't be so nasty. You know quite well that at two o'clock on Tuesday we'll all be dying at our desks trying to earn a living. Can't you make it Saturday, five o'clock?'

There is a pause. Quite a long pause. The doctor does not normally give appointments on Saturdays. But he has told this girl that he would be available any day apart from Wednesdays. Besides, Mary Thama is the sort of girl that men want to look at again and again. After a few moments, he says, 'Yes. Next Saturday at five o'clock. You know my clinic?'

'Yes. See you then.'

Jane Njeri was not interested in a boy, any boy. Not even a Doctor. She had told herself that she would keep away from anything that is remotely suggestive of falling in love. She had even managed to convince herself that falling in love is a babies' game, something for schoolgirls and schoolboys. She considered romance rather stupid. Words such as darling and sweetheart were almost comic to her. Those were foolish words. Falling in love is just one nasty joke.

But Jane had grown into a formidable experimenter. This part of her nature was not going to change. Jane still liked discovering new thrills and playing around with new ways and ideas. She was now very conscious of her beauty. She was in fact quite annoyed with herself because it had taken her so long to realise what an asset her looks were. She had wasted the best part of her life unaware of what she was capable of achieving by doing nothing other than smiling.

Saturday afternoon came. She prepared herself for a kill. She had no particular plans but she was determined to toy around with this doctor. Then she would abandon him at the crucial moment. Or maybe not, depending on how things went.

At five o'clock she was there. So was he. She sat opposite him in his clinic. He was rolled up in one of those white coats that they usually put on. She was rolled up in a demure mini and a yellow sweater that emphasised the hills and the valleys on her chest. Her right hand had two shining bangles. Some girls would have considered bangles old-fashioned but Jane Njeri liked to be different.

'You are Mary Thama, is my memory correct?' the doctor asked.

'Yes, it is. And your name is Dr Kalule. Is mine correct?'

'Yes, it is. Now Miss Thama, I would like you to get the meaning of family planning quite clear.'

'Not interested, Dr Kalule. I have no family to plan. I don't want one either, not now.'

Dr Kalule had met all types of girls before, but not one quite like this one. Being a doctor is such a good thing because you never stop learning.

'Miss Thama, perhaps you would like to hear how it all started, correct? The idea used to be called birth control, but this is not what we call it now because . . .'

'Because you do not control birth, you plan a family. But in the long run it all comes to the same thing. Fewer children. Or no children at all. Am I right?'

The doctor did not like the interruption, but what could he do? So he continued.

'Ever heard of the safe period? This is the oldest method known, apart from total abstention. Catholics like this method because no artificial gadgets are involved.'

'Yeah? But were the safe periods put there by God for family planning? You catch nature when she is helpless, stab her in the back when she is defenceless and then you go around saying that you are nature's greatest friend.'

'I like your argument, but that would not convince the Catholics. Then a man called Malthus came along. He argued that human beings were getting too many for the food available.'

'You don't have to go that far. I have read it all in books. But tell me, Doctor, when are you people going to come up with something for the men? Must it always be the women who have to do this, do that, do the other thing? I think men are selfish.'

'No, not quite, Mary, I mean Miss Thama.'

'Call me Mary.'

'The female system is regular. It comes and goes. It is therefore much easier to regulate. A man's energy is there the whole time and it is much more difficult to deal with.'

'I guess all that story was discovered by a man. Doctor, I think I should be going back home. One thing though, I have given up the pills. Every time I swallow one I hear my heart beating hard. You are correct, Doctor, these pills interfere with the heart.'

The doctor just looked at this girl. Either she was very romantic, or just crazy, or a kind of nut. He picked up courage. He decided to do something. Mary Thama must not go so soon. The doctor had to do something.

But was this not going to be too soon? After all, this was only the second time that he had met this girl, or woman, or whatever she was. He wished they had met at a social function or some place like that. He wanted to have a clean conscience as far as his professional status was concerned, but Jane Njeri was not helping him very much in that direction. He removed his white coat and hung it on a peg on the wall.

'Dr Kalule,' Jane said, 'you look very smart without that white coat of yours.'

'And now, maybe I can drop you in town. I am on my way to a meeting. I wonder why they fix these meetings at such awkward times. Six o'clock on a Saturday afternoon is quite ridiculous.'

Jane thought the doctor was trying to get rid of her in a hurry. This doctor must be a coward. He was trying his best to avoid her. Once again her dreams were shattered, simply because the man appeared to have no nerves. Why do men avoid very beautiful girls? Why does a man like this try to shake her off merely because she has flashing eyes? Was this going to be her lot in life? This looked like a puzzle without a simple solution.

'Thank you for your kind offer, Doctor. I live near Latema Road and if you would drop me anywhere near there I would be much obliged.'

The doctor was driving a flashy Peugeot car. Complete with a radio and cassettes and things. Jane Njeri made sure that the doctor got in first. Then she opened her door, raised one leg carefully and stepped in. The doctor was looking. She sat, then refused to close the door. The doctor stretched out his hand to reach for the door-handle. He was rather clumsy and his hand rubbed on Jane's chest. That was what Jane wanted. Then they got going.

'Tell me, Doctor, when you call yourself a consultant what do you mean?'

'I am a specialist.'

'In what?'

'In obstetrics and gynaecology.'

'Is that all?'

'Yes.'

'And this meeting you talked about? Not many people have meetings on Saturdays. Are you really sure you have a meeting?'

'This one is on, I assure you.'

'Where is it?'

'The Smiles Mothers' Home.'

'What about?'

'Adoption problems.'

Now Jane Njeri began feeling warm inside her. Her tongue went dry all of a sudden. Her heart began beating loudly inside her chest as if it was running on dirty kerosene. She shut up because she could not speak any more. Yes, that's how it was. Dr Donald Kalule told Jane that he was in fact the chairman of the expert committee that advises the board of the Adoption Society of Kenya on professional issues. Jane listened but said nothing.

'You can drop me near the Premier Bookshop. Thanks.'

'Good-bye, Mary. Let me know how you are getting on. You have my number.' He was really hoping that this would not be the last time.

That Saturday night Jane Njeri stayed in. She had too much on her mind to enjoy an evening out. She thought about Dr Kalule. If this doctor was connected with the Adoption Society, above all if he was associated with the Smiles Mothers' Home in any way, she was not going to let him go until he told her about her child. That was for certain.

The first thing Jane did the following Monday was to ring Dr Donald Kalule. She was going to be bold but casual. She got him on the line. They talked about the weather and such other nonsensical matters, but it was not long before she came to more personal issues. The doctor appeared to enjoy talking to her and this was very encouraging. Before long they were talking about dates.

'Doctor, how would next Saturday be?'

'O.K. with me.'

'What time?'

'As usual, five.'

'Sure you won't have a meeting this time?'

'I will, with Mary Thama.'

That was a job well done. Jane was apprehensive about what would have happened if Dr Kalule had chickened out and refused to see her. Now it only remained for her to lay down some sort of a plan in order to make the encounter productive. There was a whole week in which to do it.

But everything else around appeared to be a problem. Money, to start with, was in short supply. Good clothes and good perfumes can be expensive. Good shoes, good bedsheets, good utensils, all these things are awfully expensive. There is a bill for water and light, for groceries, for milk. No end. Seven hundred shillings may sound like a lot of money, but it does not go very far these days.

The other headache is this girl Eunice Wangeci. Fate has put them together in the same bank. She has made up her mind to ignore Jane Njeri completely. She pretends that she does not know anything about her. This is very rotten of her because she is merely putting on a show. It is odd because Jane has no ill feelings against this girl. She would like to be friendly, but the way things are, it will take some time.

But the biggest headache of all is this tall dark boy called Ali Kamau. He looks nice and handsome, but Jane has vowed to herself not to get interested in any boy. She keeps remembering what Mrs Murage told her one day. First, that the first love is unproductive. Second, that the boy who will marry her one day is likely to be somebody she has not yet met. At any rate, Jane Njeri would hate to tie herself to a boy at this stage. She wants freedom, not bondage.

This man Ali Kamau, he is really becoming a nuisance. He is very bold. He can do anything. Just imagine. The other day he came with a little envelope and dropped it dead on Jane's desk. But he did it in a very subtle way. Nobody saw him do it. And the letter?

> My lovely angel Jane,
> This is the boy who smiled at you yesterday afternoon. My heart dies for you, Jane. I think of you day and night. I love you, Jane.
> Write to me and tell me something. Anything you want.
>
> Love and Kisses,
>
> A.K.

Hear that? Same old story. All boys speak the same language. They think of the same things. And they all think that girls are so very stupid, that girls will believe in anything they are told.

Well, once upon a time, Jane was stupid. Once upon a time, she was the slave of a boy who wrote a very similar letter to her. But that was long ago. Things have changed now. Jane did not bother to reply. But she did not tear the letter up either. She pushed it into one of her boxes and left it there.

Then came Friday. Tomorrow would be the big day. Dr Donald Kalule must be made to tell the whole story. He must be made to talk. He must be made to reveal what happened on May 15th. He must be made to reveal what happened to the baby. But how?

Jane Njeri made up a little plan. She would leave him to drive to wherever he wants. But they must drink something sometime. This will make talking easier. Then Jane will try all her tricks to make this man talk. Was that a plan? Jane decided to forget all about plans. Her mind was thinking about her baby. If she played her cards right, maybe this would be her day.

On Saturday she began preparing herself at three o'clock. For about an hour and a half, she did her feminine things with the door of her flat locked. She looked at the mirror, smiled at it, looked at herself, tried various skirts. When she was over with it, any man would have said Yes.

She was at Dr Kalule's clinic at five o'clock, so was he.

'You look lovely, Mary. I must tell you, you look really lovely. Today I don't want you to call me doctor or any such funny name; just call me Donald.'

The doctor was in high spirits. It appeared as if he had had one or two doubles of something or other just to tune himself up to the correct state of mind. And was he tuned up?

This time he opened the car's door on Jane's side first. Then he got in. But the way Jane sat on that seat was such that the Doctor could not help stealing a look out of the corner of his eye. Before long he was heading for Dagoretti Corner.

'Donald, where are we heading for?'

'We shall see where the car goes to. It is Saturday, isn't it?'

Jane looked at the Ngong Hills. She was hoping that they were not going that way. She had some very unhappy memories of that place.

'Tell me about yourself, Donald. Your home area for example. Are you from Machakos?'

'No, I come from a place called Nsambya in Kampala.'

'What? You mean you are not a Kenyan?'

'No, I am a Muganda. But tribes mean nothing to me. And you, Mary?'

'I come from a place called Mugoiri in Murang'a.' A little lie quietly told cannot do nobody no harm.

The doctor told this girl about Uganda in general and in particular about Buganda. About the king of Buganda and how he was persecuted by the politicians. How he later died in London and how a number of good-looking girls were suspected of being involved.

'Every since that time, Mary, I have always been suspicious of very beautiful girls. If you live in a foreign country, you have to be careful of them.'

The doctor was of course speaking from his heart. He was completely unaware of the fact that his words would embarrass this girl. Jane was a good-looking girl and she knew it.

'You mean the beautiful ones who have no work, no doubt.'

Now the doctor woke up. 'Yes, those ones. The type that wears wigs and false eyelashes.'

'Yes, Donald. I knew this was what you meant. I hate wigs and I hate false eyelashes.'

They were now motoring along Naivasha Road and they were somewhere near the Limuru TV mast.

'Tell me, Donald, how many babies are born each month at the Smiles Mothers' Home?'

'Can't remember, Mary, just can't remember. But it is a fair number.'

Jane regretted that she had asked this question so early. She really should have waited until later on in the evening. She now thought it wise to change the topic.

'Where are we heading for, Donald? Not Kampala, I hope.'

'No, we won't pass Naivasha.'

They chatted all the way. Jane talked about her work at the bank. She said that she did not like it very much but she had met some very interesting people there. Such as Ali Kamau. Such as Eunice Wangeci.

The Doctor asked Njeri to tell him as much as possible about Ali Kamau. Jane talked freely about him. The doctor was very interested in this man. Just before getting into Naivasha, they turned left. Jane had never been in this place before. She had never seen a lake in her life and the one which was now in front of her just looked wonderful.

Before long they drove into a very large hotel situated in very pleasant surroundings. Beautiful lawns, lots of trees and of course the lake.

'Mary, would you like to go out in a boat?'

'No, I am terribly afraid of water. I can't swim. Besides, it is rather late now. I wish we had come here earlier. The view is just marvellous.'

'Those boats are very safe. They never let you down.'

Jane Njeri did not believe that there is anything safe in this world. What is there in this world that can't let you down? She had grown to be very suspicious of everything. She was now even becoming suspicious of Donald. Why, for example, did he have to come so far from Nairobi?

'Donald, why did you come all the way out here?'

Dr Kalule thought for a while. They were now near the hotel entrance. They went straight to the bar and chose a seat in the corner, away from everybody else.

'Why did we come so far? Don't you like it here?'

'It's marvellous. Besides, I have never been here before. But it is a bit expensive coming all this way for a drink.'

An attendant came in no time. Donald asked for a beer. Jane asked for brandy and ginger ale.

'No, Mary, it is not the expense that is in my mind. I want you to do something for me and I thought that this was a good place to talk about it. I want your help, Mary, I really do.'

Jane Njeri was very happy to hear this. Was the doctor really serious? Did he want to be helped? How? The usual way with men? But she would do anything for this man. So long as he was associated with the Adoption Society of Kenya, and the Smiles Mothers' Home, she would do anything for him so long as he was willing to do something for her too.

'I will do anything for you, Donald. What is it?'

'Let me give you the background information first. I am a Muganda, as I told you, from Buganda, in Uganda.'

'Yes, I know, but tribes are nothing to me.'

'What you don't know is that I am a refugee in Kenya. I had to run away from my country to avoid molestation, torture and murder.'

'Oh dear. Were you involved in politics or something?'

'That's a long story. But when I came to Kenya I got a job and I do a lot of consulting work and I am on various committees and councils. I would say that I am not doing too badly.'

'Yes? You are with the Adoption Society. Do they pay you well?'

'No, that's honorary. But consulting appointments are well paid.'

'Yeah? They are?'

'Yes, and that is the trouble.'

'Money is the trouble? If you have no money you get into trouble. If you have it you still get into trouble. But I would rather get into trouble for having too much money than for having too little.' Jane was getting philosophical.

Donald ordered another beer. Jane was still sipping her brandy.

'Some of my enemies have followed me to this country. I know them and I know where they are. These people are in the secret service.'

Dr Kalule now looked Jane Njeri straight in the eyes. This girl was beautiful all right. But she was now looking worried. Almost afraid, in fact. Definitely very uncertain of whatever was going on around her. Dr Kalule knew one or two things about beautiful girls. They can ruin a man's life, if they want to. But they can also save him from ruin and death. It all depends on how he plays his cards.

Dr Kalule was now wondering just how much he ought to tell this charming girl called Mary Thama. Should he tell her, for example, that Ali Kamau is from Uganda and that this is not his real name? Should he tell her about the gold which he and Ali smuggled from the Congo? Should he tell her about the money they got for it, the money that is still lying in a Kampala bank? He wondered.

That this money, for example, was deposited in an account belonging to both him and this man Ali. That the money could not be withdrawn unless both signed a cheque. That Ali refused to sign the very first cheque because an idea came into his head that if he killed Kalule, all that money would be his. But then Kalule has been playing with this very same idea himself. It depends on who gets whom first. It is a long story.

But Ali Kamau is the more determined. He followed Kalule all the way from Uganda to Nairobi. He has another advantage. He is a security man of some kind. Always has been. He even helps the Kenya Police in some of their investigations.

The doctor thought that he had better say something. Why not say what he wants without saying why he wants it?

'One person in particular concerns me a lot, Mary. I would like you to fix this guy. I mean, you could help me to come to terms with him.'

'No, Donald. I really do not want to be involved in this kind of thing.' Jane did not even bother to ask what 'to fix' means.

'There isn't much to it, Mary, it's quite simple. But I think I had better give you a break for a while. Have another drink.'

They had a few more drinks and then they asked for something to eat. They chose to have a full dinner.

'I find European diet rather cumbersome, Mary, don't you?'

'Why?'

'Take soup, for example. Why have you got to keep pushing the spoon away from you?'

'I really don't know. It is probably much better if you do it the other way round.'

'And this little thing called the fish course. What is the point of it?'

'To make sure that you eat fish, I suppose. Lake Naivasha is full of fish which are dying of old age.'

'I have no quarrel with the main course or the dessert. But cheese and biscuits?'

'The first time I chewed a bit of cheese I had to hold my nose,' Jane said.

'And the coffee. Tiny little bitter coffee in a tiny little cup. You know one thing, Mary, African tradition does not believe in giving somebody something in a tiny little container. It looks mean.'

'I know. But the African tradition is being eroded away by these horrid Western ways. It is crumbling and fragmenting right in front of us and not many of us are doing anything about it.'

'Mary, you sound like a culture vulture.'

'What's that? The last time I saw a vulture was in a film called "An Elephant Called Slowly".'

'You watch films a lot, then?' the doctor asked.

'Yes, Donald. Do you mean to tell me that I shouldn't watch films just because of this African tradition that we have been talking about?'

'That's the dilemma with the culture vultures. Obviously, if we accept Western materialism and technology, if we avidly go for their gadgetry and technocracy, who says that we won't have to pay a price?'

'And the price?' Jane asked.

'The erosion of a good chunk of our tradition. Look, we can't even do away with a ridiculous thing like a necktie.'

'I didn't know you were the serious type, Donald. Where do we go from here?'

'Progress has a nasty habit of heading in one direction. We are not going to discover any new ways to progress. If we want Western comforts we will find ourselves becoming slaves to those comforts like the Westerners. And that's where we are heading for, I am afraid to say.'

'Yes, but after Naivasha, what next?'

Dr Kalule looked round himself like a man waking up from a dream. He looked at Jane Njeri and smiled. She smiled back.

'I shall go inside and hire a double room. Just for you and me.'

'What's a double room?'

'It's a room with one big bed made of two little beds stuck together.'

'And what is a single room?'

'It is a room which may have two or three little beds but they are not stuck together.'

'What are the charges?'

'Ninety bob for a double, fifty for a single.'

'Well, Donald, let's take a single. If there happens to be two beds there, I'll stick them together myself.'

'But the owners may object.'

'Forget it, then. Let's go back to Nairobi. Why throw away so much money for nothing?'

Dr Donald Kalule was getting quite impressed with this girl called Mary Thama. Her drinking was moderate and her general outlook on life quite sensible. A girl who talks in terms of not throwing money down the drain is sure to impress any man.

Dr Kalule was now decided more than ever that he had found the girl whom he had always wanted. Somebody who could be used to find out one or two things about the enemies that were spying on him. But he had to be very careful not to frighten her. She definitely looked easily frightened. Perhaps they should go back to Nairobi and talk more.

'It is only one hour from here to Nairobi. Shall we get going? It is only nine o'clock now.' The doctor stood up.

They left the hotel holding hands and got going. On the way, Dr Kalule talked a lot about the problems facing developing countries. How the poor cannot rule the rich. How the strong powers will always try to influence the poor nations through their economic aid.

At times he was almost talking to himself, because Jane was not listening. She was wondering what sort of a man this was. Always talking about the serious aspects of life. This was a man who had a grudge against almost everything. Would a man like this be romantic?

Donald Kalule drove straight to his bungalow. This was situated somewhere off Ngong Road. It was a very pleasant place.

'Donald, I thought we were going to my place. Where is this?'

'This is my place. You are welcome.'

The sitting-room was very well furnished. The seats were very comfortable. The doctor came up with more drinks. There was brandy and there was beer. It also happened to be a Saturday. There was a lot of time to drink and get drunk. The doctor suggested that they take their drinks in the bedroom.'

'Who lives with you, Donald?'

'My servant.'

'And your wife?'

This was a careless question. But Kalule knew how to deal with tricky questions.

'My wife? Who told you that every man has a wife?'

Jane did not feel like pressing the point too far. That was not her worry either. Her concern at the moment was whether this was the right time to come back to the Adoption Society of Kenya. She decided to try.

'Donald, who decides which child should be adopted by whom?'

'I do, or rather, my committee does. Why?'

'I once knew a girl called Jane Njeri. We were very great friends. She became pregnant at a very early age. Relatives advised her to go to the Smiles Mothers' Home. She had a child there which was adopted. She never saw her baby.'

Jane now took a rest and gulped her brandy. She was getting a little breathless because her heart was beating faster and faster as she went deeper and deeper into the story of her own life. But the brandy did wonders for her. It calmed her down and gave her courage to proceed.

'This girl would die to know what happened to her baby. Can you help her, Donald?'

'Mary, we cannot reveal that kind of information. It is against our professional ethics.'

'Donald, I will do anything for you. Anything you want me to.'

Jane Njeri now switched her feminine charms on. She was now an expert at this kind of thing. She knew that it works wonders.

She moved closer to Donald and put her head on his lap. The doctor liked this girl because he himself had a problem to solve. The Ali Kamau problem. He was getting convinced that at last he had found the one person who might be of use to him. So long as she wanted something out of him, he would make use of her.

'Mary, I will also do anything for you. Anything you want me to,' he said.

'Then will you tell me what happened to this girl's child?'

'If I do, it will be the first time that I'll be committing a professional misdemeanour.'

'Do it for my sake, Donald. Just for my sake alone,' she pleaded.

'Yes, if you are also ready to do something for me. Something not quite so good. I gave you a hint way back at Naivasha.'

'And what is it? I am rather forgetful. I will do it whatever it is.'

Dr Kalule laughed. He was feeling good. The beer in him made him feel even better. This was a good day for him.

'Two things in fact. Mary, you will do two things for me, won't you?'

'Number one?'

'You have too many clothes on you.'

'But this light of yours is too bright.'

He switched off the overhead light and lit a dim bedside lamp.

'You mean there has to be a light on?' she asked.

'In Uganda we walk in the light.'

'I don't like light however dim it is.'

'Be bold. Be an experimenter. It will be done my way today but when we go to your flat it will be done your way. In total darkness.'

Strange people have strange habits. But Jane Njeri is a woman of strong mind. She ended up by switching off the little dim light.

'Donald, what is the other thing you want me to do?'

'I want to see Ali Kamau liquidated. You work with Ali. You

know him well. You will help me to erase him from the surface of the earth, won't you?'

'Ali Kamau? How do you know Ali Kamau? What do you mean by to liquidate? What do you mean by to erase?'

Jane Njeri was not feeling so good. The last thing she wanted was to get involved in criminal activity of any kind. Had it not been for the fact that this doctor held the secret of what had become of her child, she would never have had anything to do with this man from Uganda.

'Jane, this man called Ali Kamau is a great hypocrite. His real name is Yowasi Kizito. But he speaks Kikuyu perfectly. His Swahili is also excellent. He is very good at languages. But don't be deceived. I won't bother you with a long story about what he is doing here. But I know. I am not a fool, you know. I will never feel safe so long as Ali Kamau is in this country. You will help me to neutralise him, won't you? I will tell you what to do when the right time comes. After we have gone through with that, I will tell you anything you want to know about Jane Njeri's child. O.K.? Go ahead and get well acquainted with Ali. After that I will tell you what to do next. I wish you luck.'

For the few days that followed, Jane did her duty. She pretended to be interested in Ali Kamau. She forced herself to. That is why the whole process was so dull. But there was a purpose in it. Jane Njeri wanted to know about her child. She was ready to go through it all for this one purpose. So she befriended Ali Kamau and succeeded. Ali kept telling himself that he was the luckiest boy this side of the clouds.

One evening Ali Kamau took her to the Arboretum for a sniff of fresh air. They sat under a tree and began talking in near whispers.

'Jane, do you believe me when I tell you I love you?'

'I have always believed you, Ali. But I think that I am too young for marriage.'

'How young? How much longer would you like to wait?'

'That does not matter much, Ali. I would like us to get

acquainted with each other first. We are still strangers in a way. We work in the same place, we like each other, but I feel that we should know each other more.'

Ali said nothing. Jane said nothing. Somebody had to say something soon. Jane did.

'Tell me, how did you come to be called Ali Kamau?'

'I wish my parents were here to answer you that question, Jane. I was brought up in the Majengo slums of Nairobi, but I managed to do well at school all the same.'

'And your parents, where are they?'

'Mother is still at Majengo. Father, I don't know.'

The half-hearted talk dragged on and on. The evening came and they went to a cheap restaurant for drinks. Then they ordered something to eat. After that they proceeded to Jane Njeri's flat.

'Shall I switch off the lights, Ali?'

'No, I am used to walking in the light. But this one is too bright for me. Have you got a candle? I like something dim.'

Ali and the doctor had one thing in common. They were frightfully afraid of darkness. Perhaps all refugees are afraid of darkness. But Jane does not respect other people's phobias. She switches off all lights irrespective of whether they are dim or bright.

The following day, they both went to the bank to earn their living. People look very innocent on Monday mornings. The more innocent they look, the more hectic the week-end was.

Nobody knows where Ali Kamau lives. This man Ali is surrounded by secrets. He is surrounded by secret people too. Like the one he was talking to in a small office hidden somewhere along Tom Mboya Street in Nairobi. The man he is talking to is no other than Superintendent Kahiu Kimotho of the Kenya Police.

Superintendent Kahiu Kimotho had an interesting case on his hands. The account of the Kenya Beer Agencies has already been forged twice. On every occasion, the withdrawal signature was changed, but still, money disappeared. Two fat sums of money have already gone. The culprits are known. The problem is how to bring them to justice. The Superintendent had requested the help of Detective Assistant Yowasi Kizito, the man commonly known as Ali Kamau. The forgery took place in Ali Kamau's bank and the culprits are in that same bank.

'Superintendent Kimotho, you will agree that I have done a good job on this case.'

Ali had carried out all the investigation single-handed.

'Yes, Detective Assistant Kizito. Maybe this girl Eunice can be persuaded to come over to our side. Maybe she can tell us a lot that we still don't know.'

'I doubt it, Superintendent. I have obtained all the information I wanted from this girl. In fact, I have already ditched her. I am no longer interested in Eunice. But there is another candidate who joined the bank recently who looks promising. I am already on good terms with this girl and maybe she can help us.'

'You mean this girl Jane Njeri?'

'Yes. She is a beauty, that girl. If we could bring her over to our side, she could do some very useful work for us. Beautiful girls obtain useful information with little or no effort.'

'Then why don't you go ahead? Go and weep in front of her. Tell her you love her and all that. Write her one phoney letter after another.'

'I have already done that, Superintendent Kimotho.'

'Any results?'

'This girl is very tough but she is coming round. What girl did I ever fail to win?'

'And this Lewis Maranga chap? He is good at forgery, that boy. He has already done it twice. No wonder he has such a fat account. When shall we hand him in?'

'I have just one little job left to do. I like hot evidence, Superintendent Kimotho. You know me. I don't like doing things by halves. I think I will catch them red-handed. I am out for a masterpiece.'

'Beautiful. But see that they do not slip away before they are in the net. Let me know when it is done. Care for a drink? Let's drive out to Thika. I like that place called the "Long Horn".'

At Makadara, Eunice Wangeci and Lewis Maranga were making the final arrangements for their wedding.

'Eunice, I didn't know that a wedding could be so expensive,' Lewis said.

'It's bound to be, because you want too many parties. One for my parents at Uthiru, another one for your parents at Ihithe, still another one for your friends at Nairobi. Lewis, why don't we scratch all these parties and save the money?'

'Marriage comes once, to most people I mean. Besides, money is not a problem. After two clean jobs, why worry about money? You know what I mean, don't you?'

Yes, Maranga had already done it twice. The bank account of the Kenya Beer Agencies had twice been withdrawn by an unknown person. The first time he did it with the help of Thuo Thenge, the clerk in charge of the records. They did it like professionals. Thuo produced the card with the withdrawal signature. Lewis Maranga traced out the signature. He knew where to get a blank cheque from, a Kenya Beer Agencies cheque. It was worth ten thousand, that job. That was before Eunice joined the bank. That was the fat money which Eunice saw in Maranga's account when she joined the bank.

Eunice Wangeci was involved with the second job. She is the one who took the card from Thuo. She is the one who traced out the signature. Eunice is not the type of girl that would run away from good money. They made fifteen thousand the second time.

'Eunice, I asked you whether you understand me.'

'Oh yes, dear, I do. Whoever taught you these tricks? You know, I was quite afraid of doing it the last time.'

'Darling, we must buy a new car the day after our wedding.'

'Good idea. A new car for our honeymoon is exactly what we need.'

'But we are rather low on money. Remember the plot we are thinking of buying? And the wedding costs? The dowry, the goats, the cows, the beer? And the new car we want to buy? I have an idea at the back of my mind.'

'I know what idea you have. But I would not like us to do it again. I know of a man who . . .'

'Now, darling, why do you want to chicken out at the most crucial time? Frankly, I hardly required the money on the first two occasions. But this time I need money badly. Will you or will you not?'

'Let me finish my story first. I knew of a man who was in charge of a big detention camp. He made sure that all the provisions for the detainees came from his own farm. He also happened to be in charge of accounts and so he used to add a few zeros here and there, you know what I mean. He became very rich. But then he received a transfer notice. A very lucky guy he was, because if he had been transferred without any queries being raised, it would have been very difficult to charge him once he was away.'

'So what happened?'

'He did it once more. Just once more. For the very last time. He changed three hundred to eight hundred and four thousand into forty thousand.'

'Precisely. The pen is mightier than the sword.'

'But this time he was nabbed. He is now cooling his heels at Shimo-la-Tewa Prison. I think he got seven years for it.'

They both laughed. Lewis Maranga has a hoarse, unenthusiastic laugh. Eunice Wangeci laughs with her cheeks drawn back and her eyes staring out into space.

'Now my question, darling. Will you or will you not?' Maranga asked.

She hesitated. Some people talk about feminine intuition. Maybe this was what was now at play. Eunice just kept quiet.

'Speak up, Eunice. All you have to do is to wait for the card from Thuo Thenge and trace out the new signature. Even my old grandmother could do that. And don't forget what I intend buying for you. A diamond ring, if you want, or a very flashy pair of pants. So please open up your mouth and talk.'

Eunice Wangeci still would not talk. It was a difficult decision to make. She really did not want to do it but there was no way out.

'Darling,' she said, 'must I do it?'

'Yes, dear, you must. Just once more. You have only done it once, and it was a good job. A good job should never be done once, it should be done at least twice. Now, darling, will you or will you not?'

Eunice now gave way. 'I will do it,' she said.

6

Bwana Absalom and his wife Agatha were quite happy with their only daughter who was now in Nairobi. Not only was she a tall, beautiful and healthy girl, but she was an intelligent and obedient child. She was also religious and very concerned with the matters of the soul. Above all, she had sailed through her education effortlessly, unlike many girls in the village who did not seem to do well at all. Gideon Murage had told them that Jane had a good job in Nairobi.

But Jane Njeri was their only child. Way back when she used to go to school at Ihithe, Agatha saw her daughter in the morning, at lunchtime and in the evening. But not so now.

She had already finished her education and she was now working. Before long, she would get married and disappear from home completely.

Agatha knew the joys of having a child in the family. She now had a great urge to have another child. Just a child, any child. She knew that she was getting on in years. She wanted one before she was too old.

But those who knew Agatha marvelled at the way she was growing old slowly. Women of her age were already wizened up. But not so with Agatha. There must be a reason. Perhaps women whose bodies are not subjected to the experience of constant childbearing can keep young for many years. It's a kind of compensation for their misfortune.

She thought of her loneliness for many days. Her loneliness was killing her, but what could she do? Ultimately she thought she had an answer. But would her husband like her plan? One day she tried to find out.

'Bwana Absalom, I do not think that we should be lonely like this,' she said. 'We are not poor people although we are not rich. Too much loneliness is not good for the mind nor for the heart. We need a child to look after. A child to transfer fatherly and motherly love to. We have a lot of unspent energy in our hearts. We need a child to make us have a full and a rich life.'

'Agatha, why do you talk like this? Why do you talk like a person who does not know about our past life? The good Lord gave us only one child. Who are we to criticise Him for not giving us another?'

'No, Absalom, we will not criticise the Lord. All we shall do is to glorify Him by looking after one of His children. By looking after another child.'

'Explain.'

'We can adopt a child. An unwanted child. The child would be our own child by law. We would cherish it and love it. We would look after it and watch it grow. It would be our joy and happiness. Above all, these lonely evenings would be lonely no more. I would be busy during the day and during the night like all women are. Our old age would be a beauty to behold. Our . . .'

'Just a second, Agatha. Give me a chance. How would you like to bring up a child who is not yours? I am not quite sure myself whether I would like to be called the father of a child who is not really mine. There is something improper about it somewhere. Something unnatural. What do you think, Agatha?'

'But what is that compared to the service that we would be offering to God? Preparing a soul for Heaven?'

Bwana Absalom thought about this proposition for a few days.

The idea was rather strange to him. He had heard about adoptions many times but he did not know of anybody who had an adopted child. But Agatha's argument was forceful and logical. He did not want to be a stumbling-block where his wife's happiness was concerned. In the end, Absalom agreed to adopting a child.

'Agatha, I agree with you that we should adopt a child. But how do we got about it?' he asked.

'We shall register ourselves with the Adoption Society of Kenya. We will tell them of our requirements. They will call us for an interview. They will come and inspect our home to satisfy themselves that the child will live in a comfortable home. Then we shall wait until they have a suitable child. They will bring it right here to our door.'

'And the legal side of it?'

'We need not worry about that. We shall ask one of the lawyers at Nyeri to process the matter on our behalf.'

'All right, Agatha. You may go ahead and fix it. And if they have two babies instead of one, let's have two.'

Agatha Waceke went ahead with the arrangements. She was absolutely delighted with the prospect of having a child at home. And she hoped this child would do a lot of crying and a lot of laughing like other children do.

Within a few weeks, Agatha and Absalom found themselves in front of the Board of the Adoption Society of Kenya. The Chairman of the Board was an old European. He was a retired Magistrate. Agatha did all the talking. Absalom did all the listening.

'Have you any other children?'

'Only one. A girl of eighteen years. She has already finished school.'

'Have doctors ever told you why you are unable to have another child?'

'No. We take this as the will of the Lord.'

'What sex would you prefer?'

'Male.'

'Any particular reason?'

'Because the other one is a girl.'

'And when can we come round to inspect your home?'

'Any time.'

Agatha and Absalom went back home. They waited and waited. Days passed, months passed. But at long last, an inspector came. He looked outside the house. He looked inside. Then he went back.

One cool morning, the baby came. When the Adoption Society of Kenya says that they will bring you a baby, that's what they do. This was a brand-new boy, only a few days old. Delicate, with nice scanty hair and small red lips.

Agatha Waceke was given a lot of instructions on how to look after this delicate thing. How to dilute cow's milk, how to use the feed bottle, how to wash napkins, which powders to use. She knew a lot of this herself but a little reminding did her no harm.

And about the baby itself? Only one piece of information was provided. The certificate of birth. Children these days are rather fond of birthday parties.

This new baby changed Bwana Absalom's home completely. There was loneliness no more. Agatha was the happiest woman for miles around, and she had every reason to be.

You would have thought that with a good, steady job, Jane Njeri would now settle down into a regular, dull life. The sort of life most of us lead. Up in the morning, off to work, back in the evening, on to some unappetising supper and off to bed. But not quite. Ali Kamau wouldn't let her. He had his own plans. One evening, for example, he went to see her in her flat with some very enticing news.

'How would you like to earn one thousand shillings in a matter of minutes?'

'I can't earn one thousand shillings in a matter of minutes, Ali. You know I can't. Even you, you can't. If you could, you would be a rich man.'

'I can't, Jane, but you can. Don't look so surprised.'

Ali explained in great detail what he wanted Jane Njeri to do for him. It was not very complicated. Jane agreed to carry out those instructions to the finest detail.

'That's fine, but what is the point in all this? Am I supposed to do things blindly without knowing what is really behind it all? Like a fool?'

'Jane, if you want to earn one thousand shillings for a five-minute job, you must be prepared to ask no questions.'

Jane understood. She was not going to ask any questions. Ali's instructions were simple and clear, and the money was good.

Eunice and Lewis will be married this coming Saturday. The cards were sent out ages ago. Even Jane Njeri has one. She has no ill feelings in her heart. She is ready to see Lewis Maranga get married to Eunice Wangeci. It has happened before. How many girls have seen their former boy-friends getting married to strange girls? Jane Njeri will definitely be attending this wedding. She has even chosen her present.

Grace Wangare and Bethwell Mbarathi would be there too. They would be playing the role of bridesmaid and best man. Eunice was reluctant at first to have a girl like Grace taking such top honours as being her bridesmaid, but it was either her or else Bethwell would be out as well.

At Uthiru, where the marriage ceremony was to be held, all was ready. There was plenty of food for all. But no beer. Drinking beer is evil if you are saved in the Lord. Eunice's parents are staunch Christians. But the crowds that were expected to gather here would certainly be well fed. Lewis Maranga had paid a lot of dowry. He had the money. His parents-in-law had nothing to worry about. It was one of the very few occasions when all the dowry had been paid before marriage.

It was much the same story at Ihithe. But it was not going to be dry in this place. Lewis Maranga's parents are not such staunch Christians as the folks at Uthiru. At Ihithe there would be native hooch, a lot of bottled beer, and who knows, even a little gin, brandy and whisky.

Lewis Maranga was now on leave in order to finalise his marriage affairs. He was in a permanent state of drunkenness. His coming marriage was too exciting for him. At the bank they would not give Eunice one week's leave before Saturday as she wanted. She would only be free from Thursday afternoon, but she would have five weeks after marriage. She was not much worried about this, though. She did most of her preparations in the evenings and she was quite happy with the progress she had made so far.

Bethwell Mbarathi was looking into the Nairobi drinks party. It would be held at the Kaloleni Social Hall. What Bethwell organises always succeeds. Naturally, Eunice and Lewis were now looking forward to their big day.

'Eunice, do you know what will happen next Saturday?'

'I will become your wife. You will become my husband.'

'Are we all set for it?'

'Yes.'

'No. Have you thrown away all your pills?'

'Oh dear, oh dear.'

She delved into her handbag and pulled them out. She threw them on the charcoal burner. They burned rather reluctantly, with a nauseating, objectionable odour.

'Good. The other job is tomorrow, Thursday. Friday is a good day to cash that cheque. On my wedding day, my pockets will be full of money. Mr Moneybags, that's what they will call me at the church. In fact, I think I will give the clergyman two thousand shillings if he plays his game well, especially if he is quick and short. I have seen clergymen taking half a day to preach to wedding couples. It certainly used to happen at Ihithe where I come from. There used to be a certain Bwana Absalom who would talk until people went to sleep. I hope things will be different at Uthiru. I really do.'

Thursday was just like any other day at the Bank. Thuo Thenge was at his records desk as usual. Ali Kamau was doing his calculations upstairs. Eunice Wangeci was doing her typing and shorthand for Mr Munyi as she had always done. Jane Njeri was at her place downstairs sorting out bills and invoices and credits and debits.

Ten o'clock is coffee time at the bank. For the people at the counters, it makes no difference whether it is coffee time or not. They are simply too busy. But not so for many others, especially the senior officers. They relax a little and chat with their friends. Others go to the other corner of the building to say a quick hello to their colleagues. But for Thuo Thenge, this was time for business. Today, especially.

He pulled out the signature card of the Kenya Beer Agencies. His hands were trembling. This was odd because on the other two occasions he had not trembled. He put it in an envelope and pushed it into his pocket. He then casually walked upstairs to Eunice Wangeci's desk. He handed her the envelope.

Eunice smiled and hid the card among the masses of paper on her desk. Thuo Thenge whispered, 'Don't take too long, Eunice. I want it back in half an hour.' He then went back downstairs to his place of work.

Eunice carefully put the card in her handbag. Her hands were sweating a little but that could have been due to the heat in the place. She left for the toilets. There, she placed a transparent piece of paper on the card and obtained a very good tracing of the signature. She made two more tracings just to make sure. She put the tracings in her handbag and then walked back to her desk. The whole operation took her less than a quarter of an hour.

Back at her desk, Eunice began fidgeting and cursing inside her. Why was Thuo taking so long to come for the card? Must he wait until a complete half-hour is over? Should she go downstairs and give the card back to him? Or should she fling the thing out through the window?

In the meantime, Ali Kamau had given Jane Njeri a prearranged signal. Jane had been waiting for this signal for the whole of last week and this one. She was glad that at last the crucial moment had arrived. The moment to earn one thousand shillings.

She picked up her handbag and went upstairs. She was at Eunice Wangeci's desk just when the latter was fidgeting and cursing. When Eunice saw Jane Njeri coming towards her, she almost howled. The two did not talk often, although they exchanged the occasional cool hello.

Jane Njeri placed her handbag next to Eunice Wangeci's according to instructions. Then she tried to engage Eunice in a conversation.

'Eunice, I was so glad to receive the invitation to your wedding,' she said.

'Many thanks, Jane. Please do sit down. How are things with you?'

'So – so, Eunice. I hope you won't mind if I don't come to Uthiru. I would like to go to Ihithe and have my share of rejoicing there. Did I ever tell you that I come from Ihithe, same as your husband-to-be?'

'Yes, you did. Let's see you at Ihithe when we get there. We should be there on Saturday at about four in the afternoon.'

'O.K., Eunice. Wish you all the luck.'

Jane picked up the wrong handbag and left. She went straight out of the bank and into Tom Mboya Street. She had been shown where Superintendent Kahiu Kimotho's little office was. She knocked. The door opened.

'I am Jane Njeri. I want to see Number Four.'

Superintendent Kimotho answered and said, 'I am Number Four. Quick, give me the handbag.'

He opened the handbag and removed one or two things from it, using a pair of forceps. He was very careful not to touch anything by hand.

'Good. Let us now go back to the bank,' he said.

They walked back in a hurry. Even Jane was now sweating. She was not used to this kind of thing. But she did not want to lose that one thousand shillings. She was almost through with the job anyway.

'Jane, do you remember what to say when we get back?' Superintendent Kimotho wanted to be sure.

'Yes I do. "Is this your handbag Eunice?" Correct?'

'Correct.'

Eunice Wangeci was now looking at her watch. Thuo Thenge would be coming for the card any minute now. He really should not have waited for so long, but so long as he came in the end, all would be well.

At last he came. But behind him there were two other people, Jane Njeri and another tall man in ordinary clothes. Eunice Wangeci looked at this man. If this is what Njeri had chosen for a boyfriend, then she had better go back to the market. There is bound to be something better somewhere. This bloke does not even have a tie on. And this is a bank, one of the most respectable banks in the whole country.

Jane Njeri made sure that she spoke before Thuo did. She knew what to say.

'Eunice, is this your handbag?' Jane was now hoping that she had used the correct formula. She was also very glad that her part was now over.

'Oh, yes, it is, Jane. This is my handbag. You must have taken it by mistake.'

Thuo Thenge was the most puzzled man around. He was wondering how handbags came into the story. He was wondering what this very good-looking girl and the tall fellow were doing there. He was burning to get back his card to put it back into the cabinet. Supposing, just supposing that somebody from the Kenya Beer Agencies wanted to withdraw money this very moment.

'Eunice, can I have it?' Thuo was certain that nobody would know what he was talking about.

Eunice Wangeci opened her handbag and began looking for the card. She searched for a minute or two then looked up in bewilderment. The thing was not there.

Superintendent Kimotho now came into the picture, and in style too.

'Eunice Wangeci and Thuo Thenge. My name is Superintendent Kahiu Kimotho. I am a senior officer of the Kenya Police Force and here is my identification.'

He showed both of them his Force card. I doubt whether they

were able to see it properly. They were sweating profusely and their mouths were as dry as the stones at Moyale. General confusion was reigning supreme in their minds.

'You are both under arrest.' He handcuffed both of them.

At this point, Jane Njeri melted away quietly. People were beginning to get interested in what was happening. Luckily, Eunice Wangeci's desk was in a little room by itself and it was not easy for the bank staff to see what was going on.

But a good many people saw the two captives being led downstairs. Eunice Wangeci was still clutching her handbag. It was a sorry sight. I wish Superintendent Kimotho had chosen another day. Such as last year or the year before. Or three or four years after Eunice Wangeci's wedding. But the ways of the law and the ways of the Lord have one thing in common. They are both as decisive as they are mysterious.

There was a car waiting outside. Just an ordinary car. Eunice and Thuo disappeared into it. Superintendent Kimotho did not accompany them. He casually turned about and went back on foot to his little office on Tom Mboya Street. Immediately he got there, he grabbed the phone. He called his Assistant Chief Inspector Kiruhi Mwania.

'There is a lovely bird coming. She is accompanied by the most brilliant records officer at the bank. Have you pulled in the bird's mate?'

'Yes, sir, we have.'

'These two were to get married next Saturday, as you know. You better do them a favour and hurry up things in general.'

'Definitely, sir. They will be in Court tomorrow morning.'

Jane Njeri was not feeling quite so good. Her heart was feeling awful. Maybe what she had done was going to put a lot of people into a lot of trouble. She was feeling what Judas Iscariot felt one day. She looked around her to see whether there was anything that would distract her mind. There was. A telephone. She called Dr Donald Kalule. They had a very long conversation. That same evening, Jane went to see Dr Kalule. They talked and talked.

This helped her to forget what happened during the day. But the Doctor had his problems too. This is a strange world. He talked about his money in Kampala. The problem was how to get at it.

Eunice Wangeci found herself in a small room at the Western Police Station. Her handcuffs were removed and she was shown to a chair near a table. Facing her sat a young man who hardly looked eighteen but he could have been twenty or over. Her interrogator definitely looked handsome.

Eunice Wangeci was given some sort of a warning that she need not say anything if she didn't want to but if she did talk whatever she said might be used in evidence against her. It all sounded very strange.

'Your name is Eunice Wangeci. Your home is at Uthiru. You are Lewis Maranga's fiancée, right?'

'Yes.' She saw little use in keeping quiet or trying to be obstructive. An idea now crossed her mind that she ought to ask for a lawyer.

'I would like to see a lawyer,' she said. 'I think I am entitled to one.'

'You don't need to throw your good money down the drain. If you tell us the truth, you will not need a lawyer.'

'How do you mean?'

'Just tell us the truth and you will never see the inside of a Court of Law. There's a racket that's going on and we think that you can help us. All we want is to get the truth out of your lungs. If we are satisfied, you will walk out of here a free girl.'

This was good news for Eunice. She was now ready to tell them anything they wanted provided they would let her go.

'I am ready to tell you the whole truth. But what about Lewis Maranga? Have you done anything to him?' Eunice was already suspecting that Lewis might also have been arrested.

'All I can tell you, Eunice, is that if you help us, we will try our best to help him.'

'You want a confession from me, don't you?' she said.

'No, we don't want a confession of any kind, just the truth. Tell us, for example, about this morning.'

He removed the traced signatures from his pocket and placed them in front of her. He showed her the signature card.

'These, for example. They were removed from your handbag.'

Eunice bit her lips. She cursed Jane and cursed her again. She regretted that she had allowed herself to be dragged into all this. A disorganised idea about her marriage ran across her mind and her tongue went cold. She forgot to answer the question.

'Eunice, look at these traced signatures. As I told you, they were taken from your handbag this morning. What have you got to say?'

'I traced them. Thuo Thenge asked me to.'

'You have done this once before, haven't you?'

This was too much for Eunice. Do these people know everything? Who told them all this? Would there be any point in being secretive? She started sobbing.

The police officer gave her time, plenty of time. He just watched her sob quietly and waited until she stopped.

'Now, Eunice, you have done this once before, haven't you?'

'Yes. Only once before.'

'That is all. No more questions. Please wait here for a short time.'

He disappeared and locked the door. After about a quarter of an hour, he came back with a statement.

'Read this, Eunice. If it is an accurate record of what you told me, you can sign it. Your agreeing to sign it must of course be purely voluntary.'

He sat and watched her read it. It was a very short statement. It was a simple, straightforward repetition of what she had already said. She signed it.

'Thank you very much, Eunice. I am going to release you now. But remember that you have committed an offence in law. Forgery is a very serious offence and if convicted of it you could go to jail for quite a long stretch. Can you do one more thing for me, Eunice?'

'What?'

'Go to your Ngara flat and stay there. Don't go out until a police officer tells you to. You can obtain whatever provisions you want from Maina Menyu's shop downstairs. It is better to lock yourself in your own room than to be locked up by somebody else in a police cell, isn't it?'

Lewis Maranga was locked up in a different room within the same police station. The same interrogator now went to him and showed him Eunice Wangeci's statement.

'You know that signature, don't you?' he asked.

'Yes, I do.'

'Have you got anything further to add?'

He had. He told about the first forgery. How he had obtained the blank cheques. He told about the second and third forgeries. In short, he spilled the beans nice and proper. What can you do if your girl-friend shoots out her mouth as if the world was coming to an end? He signed a statement.

Thuo Thenge was next. He was shown the two statements. He read them very calmly. This boy was tough. I think he should have joined the army.

'You produced the cards on the three occasions, didn't you?'

'No.'

'Who else could have done it apart from you?'

'I don't know.'

'Nobody else operates that section of the records department apart from you?'

'The bank management knows the answer to that question.'

'This morning you were seen going to Eunice Wangeci's desk at ten o'clock.'

'Somebody must have been seeing things. The age of miracles is not yet over. Even the best of us sometimes have hallucinations.'

'We have witnesses who saw you give Eunice the card. You told her that you wanted it back in half an hour.'

'Yeah? Were you there?'

'No, but Eunice was. It's in her statement, sir.'

'Yeah? Is Eunice infallible?'

'Another thing: who said "Eunice, can I have it?" Do you recall anybody using those words this morning?'

'How can I recall what every chatterbox was saying in the bank this morning or any other morning for that matter?'

'Because those words were recorded. Can I play the whole conversation back to you? Your mind definitely requires a little refreshing.'

The police officer locked the room and left. He came back with a small box that looked like a radio. He touched a few knobs here and there and the thing began talking. Thuo Thenege now began sweating profusely. This day should have been called Sweating Thursday.

'If you are ready to co-operate, the police will definitely take this into account. Your two colleagues have been very helpful.'

Thuo softened down. He agreed to be helpful. He spilled the beans nice and proper. He told his story, then signed a statement.

The following morning, Lewis Maranga and Thuo Thenge appeared in Court charged with forgery and issuing forged documents. The prosecution was careful to mention that both had been co-operative and had helped the police in their investigations.

The boys pleaded guilty. The Court was adjourned for sentence later on in the morning. At a quarter past eleven, the Court reconvened. The two were sentenced to four years in prison. That Friday evening, Lewis Maranga was cooling his heels at Kabete Jail. Thuo Thenge was taken to Kitale Prison.

Superintendent Kimotho went to Ngara that Friday evening. He knew where Eunice lived. Upstairs, on top of Maina Menyu's head, that's where. He knocked.

'Who's that?' she asked anxiously.

'Superintendent Kimotho of the Kenya Police.'

She opened. He moved in and closed the door behind him. He could see that her eyes were swollen. They were also quite red.

'Eunice, I have come here to see whether there is anything else we can do to help you.'

'You brutes, you cruel animals of the bush. You did not release my Maranga. You are still locking him up. You know how cruel this is. You know . . .'

'Calm down, Eunice. One good turn deserves another. I am here to help. Remember that we let you go only because you were ready to help us. Now, can I be of any further help or shall I go back?'

'Tell me what happened to Maranga.'

'I really don't know. I was not in the Court.'

'How much money was he fined?'

'It is not likely that he got away with a mere fine. Forgery is a very serious offence.'

Superintendent Kimotho now paused and looked round the room. Small, but quite well kept. He was calculating. Is this the proper moment to do what he had come here to do? He decided to try.

'Eunice, would you like us to take you to Mombasa tonight? You have five weeks' leave. It shouldn't be difficult for you to get a stenographer's job at Mombasa. You can write a notice of resignation once you get there. Shall we take you down to Mombasa or shall we not?'

'Take me,' she said.

The Superintendent obliged. Eunice Wangeci was off to Mombasa that same evening.

It wasn't the first time that a wedding has had to be cancelled. Normally, when this happens, it is for an understandable reason. For example, the groom might chicken out because he is scared stiff of the prospect of sleeping in the same bed with a female. Or the bride might deliver a baby on the morning of the wedding. But this time things were a little out of the way.

Naturally, there was panic and general confusion. At Uthiru, special prayers were said. It took some time for the news to get to Ihithe, but when it did arrive, most people were too drunk to care.

Some of them in fact did not know whose wedding this was supposed to be, anyway.

The Nairobi party, however, was never held. Bethwell Mbarathi drove out with Grace Wangare to a place called Njabini. That's where they spent the week-end. That's where they went to forget everything. They roast their meat very nicely at Njabini and the meat there has never seen the inside of a refrigerator. As it simmers on a charcoal grill, it emits the odour of roast meat as it used to be before they discovered coolers and freezers. Besides, the view of the Aberdares from there is just wonderful. And there was beer too. Good cold beer. At Njabini, they never freeze their beer. It just cools itself off and waits for a thirsty throat to come and gurgle it. Such as Bethwell's.

On the following Saturday evening, Jane Njeri was with Ali Kamau. They were hidden in a corner at the 'Three Swallows'. It was about seven in the evening and they were having a few drinks. It was the first time they had been in this place together.

'Once upon a time, Jane, I saw you in this very place. You were chatting with a dame who looked married and well settled down.'

'How did you know?'

'Rings on her fingers. I am an eagle when it comes to looking. I am a computer when it comes to remembering.'

'And you are an elephant when it comes to drinking,' she said.

'Sure, like today. It's a Saturday, isn't it? And I have a dry throat and a tummy, haven't I?'

'Ali, darling, today you are in such high spirits. It is not often that I have seen you so relaxed, so happy, so totally in harmony with the environment.'

'My happiness is infectious, Jane, isn't it? Or shall I cheer you up dear? I must turn you on.'

Ali put his hands into his pockets and came out with a thick wad of the pinkest notes you ever saw. He placed them in Jane Njeri's lap. They were hidden away in a corner and it was not easy for the other patrons to see what was going on between them.

'Count that and put it into your handbag. That's yours. Have you forgotten?'

It was one thousand shillings, Jane's reward for doing a good job.

'Yesterday, Jane, I just couldn't get you. I was ready for a drink after last Thursday's Operation Forgery. Did you forget that I promised you something?'

'I didn't really forget but at the same time I didn't want to do anything in a hurry. Where was I on Thursday? At home.'

Which was a lie. She was with Dr Kalule. They were laying down the plan for this evening.

'That evening I was all alone. And yesterday? Where were you yesterday evening?' Ali's speech was a little unsteady.

'I was feeling awful. I went to bed at eight o'clock.' Which was true because she had a terrible conscience. She had to go to bed to forget everything.

'Forget it, dear, let's drink,' he said.

'Ali, thanks for the fifty quid. At first I thought you were joking.'

'Joking? Me? When did I joke last?'

'When you talked of walking in the light.'

'Forget it. Today I am so drunk I couldn't, even with the studio lights on.'

'Then go ahead and get drunk, Ali. I will look after you properly. I have more than one thousand shillings in my handbag just now. It's easy money and we might as well see whether we can finish it. Can we finish it, dear?'

'You joke with me? Just give me half a chance. And if you call one thousand shillings a lot of money, you don't know what a lot of money is. If you knew how much I pocketed out of that job, your heart would beat like the Ashanti drums.'

'Then don't tell me, Ali. Today is not quite the best day for a coronary. I have a job to do. I must look after you.'

And so it went on. Drinking, talking, cracking nasty jokes, getting drunk.

'Jane, you are not drunk. What's the matter?'

'We should not both get drunk.'

The music played and they went and danced. Ali was not dancing well. Then they came back and had more drinks. The music played again. Ali excused himself to go to the toilet. Jane opened her handbag and pulled out a small bottle. She released the cap. She took his glass, sat facing the wall so that nobody could see what she was about to do and poured the contents of the bottle into Ali's beer. The bottle did not contain much of anything. Just a pinch of a white substance. Then she put everything back into position and just sat there.

Ali came from the toilet, held her hand and led her to the dancing floor. This time Ali's dancing was atrocious. Too much drink is not good for anything. Jane was much relieved when the music stopped playing at last.

They went back to their table. Ali took his beer and emptied the glass.

'Jane, give me some more. That last glass must have gone kind of stale. It is making my stomach shift up and down. And while we are at it, I hereby declare that I will dance no more.'

So they just sat there drinking and watching people dance. The world around them was noisy and uninteresting. Quite a good number of people at the 'Three Swallows' appeared totally uninterested in life, in drinking, in music. They had come to this place just because it happened to be a Saturday, as if to do something which they were duty bound to do.

After half an hour or so, the first symptoms began coming. Donald Kalule was right because he said that the bloke would begin by sweating profusely. Which is what he was doing just now. But he was not correct when he said that he would open his mouth next. Ali refused to do it. He chose to do things his own way. He collapsed on the table. The table tilted towards him. He fell on the floor and the table came on top of him. The drinks were spilled all over the place. The glasses broke into tiny little fragments.

What followed next could only be described as general

confusion. The band stopped playing. People rushed hither and thither as if unable to make up their minds what to do. Somebody went to the phone and dialled three nines. Then he called an ambulance. Another one came to Ali and began to fan him. Another one came with a pail half full of water and poured it all on the poor man's head.

The owner of the 'Three Swallows', an elderly European, was now getting very concerned about the sequence of events. He had never had a customer collapse in his place before and he was not quite certain whether it was his responsibility to take the man to hospital or not. He would certainly have to do something if the police or the ambulance failed to come soon.

He went and stood at the door, watching to see whether the police or the ambulance was on the way. Yes, a police patrol car was coming. He could hear the siren. Then the car appeared.

He went back into the bar. 'The police car is here. Bring him outside,' he shouted.

Three drunks offered their services. They raised Ali up. Then they made for the door. But Ali Kamau was not quite as light as these drunks thought. Either that, or else the three drunks were not as strong as they thought they were. After they had taken a few steps, Ali slipped and fell back to the floor, hitting the ground with his head first. It wasn't a good day for Ali, this one, it definitely wasn't.

'Leave him alone,' somebody shouted, 'just leave him alone. He may have fractured his skull. The police are here. They will look after him.'

The police came and carried him gently to the car and drove off to the hospital.

Jane Njeri quietly left the 'Three Swallows' and went and locked herself up in her flat. She tried to forget everything that had happened that evening. It was all too much for her. A confusion of emotions went through her whole system. She became sick and fed up with everything. There was only one good thing she could do, to cry. And that is what she did.

On Sunday morning, Superintendent Kimotho was awakened by the loud ringing of his home telephone. It sounded louder than usual. Acting Assistant Commissioner Morris Mrefu was on the line.

'Superintendent, I am sorry to wake you up so early. Detective Assistant Yowasi Kizito died last night in hospital. This is a big blow to us because he was extremely useful. The matter is now in your hands.'

'Yes, sir.'

Before long, all sorts of people were making statements. The owner of the 'Three Swallows' made a particularly long statement. The three drunks who carried Ali Kamau did the same, but this time they were perfectly sober. They all described Jane Njeri in similar terms, tall, fair, beautiful, very intimate with this man.

At about ten o'clock on Sunday morning, Superintendent Kimotho was knocking at Jane Njeri's flat.

'Come in.'

'So it's you, Njeri. We were together just a few days ago, weren't we? Must be last Thursday. Correct?'

'Quite correct, Number Four. Take a seat, Superintendent. Last Thursday our meeting was very short, wasn't it?

'Quite correct. But this time it won't be. We are going to sit together here for quite some time.'

Jane Njeri now switched on her courage. She knew that she could have nerves of steel if she chose to, but the problem was that courage did not always come when the need was there. Like now.

'I am investigating the death of Ali Kamau, your colleague at the bank.'

'Is he dead? I am so sorry to hear it. I am really so very sorry. He was a very great friend of mine.'

'Jane, we are fully aware of the fact that you helped us tremendously in investigating the forgeries at your bank. I am equally certain that you will be helpful to us in this case. Ali was friendly with a lot of people and we have a duty to see that the cause of his death is established as soon as practicable. Now, you were with Ali last night, weren't you?'

'Yes, I was.'

'Did he have a lot to drink?'

'He did. He was very drunk. But I was not. I did not want both of us to get drunk.'

'What happened? Tell me in your own words how it all started.'

'He collapsed on the table, then fell down. The table also fell and the glasses got broken. Beer was spilled all over the place. The police were called. They came. Three people volunteered to carry him to the car outside but they dropped him. His head hit the floor. The police took him to the car.'

'Is that all?'

'Yes.'

'Is there any other information you know which might help us with this investigation?'

'No.'

With that, Superintendent Kimotho left. Jane Njeri was happy to see him go. He went back to his little office on Tom Mboya Street which was not far from Njeri's flat. He grabbed the phone and called his boss.

'All the key witnesses have now been interviewed, sir.'

'Are you making any arrests? This girl, for example, what about her?'

'I cannot get much sense out of her story, sir, although she appears to be telling the truth, though not necessarily, the whole truth.'

'Then lock her up, Superintendent, lock her up.'

'If it turns out to be poisoning, I will definitely lock her up.'

But it did not turn out to be poisoning. The cause of death was officially stated as being due to cerebral haemorrhage. The skull was found to have been fractured and many blood vessels in the brain were ruptured. So Jane Njeri was not locked up. But the three drunks were, the three drunks who dropped their cargo.

The glass fragments were collected by the police. They were also careful to collect as much liquid as possible from the floor by soaking it up with clean cloth. These items would be analysed for poison. An analysis would also be carried out on Ali's body to find out whether he had taken poison. This would take some time. The results, however, would be crucial to the case. Superintendent Kimotho could therefore do nothing decisive until he saw the analyst's report.

But Jane Njeri did a lot of things that were decisive. That Sunday morning, she swore to herself never again to get involved in crime and murder. She decided to mind her own business from that day onwards. The only thorn in her side was the fact that she still knew nothing about her child. But she was determined to wash her hands and to go back to a straight life once more. But how?

By writing a letter to her bank. A letter of resignation. She gave them the usual one month's notice. She would leave this bank completely and look for another job elsewhere. Anywhere.

Then she thought of something else to do. Something crazy. As crazy as resigning, or even worse. She wrote another letter to the headmistress of the Kitui Women's Teacher Training College, applying for a place. She told her a long story about how she had always wanted to be a teacher. She enclosed copies of all her certificates. Just in case she changed her mind later on in the day, she went and posted both letters there and then. If that wasn't a decisive action, I don't know what is.

Jane thought that Dr Kalule would ring her up on Sunday or Monday. But he didn't. This was strange because she had carried out his instructions well. He did not ring her on Tuesday either. She made up her mind to go and see him on Wednesday evening. Which she did.

She got there at about seven o'clock. The doctor was there. He was looking great and generally very pleased with himself. Either that or else the Beefeater Gin which he had just been drinking was doing its work.

'Cheer up, Mary, cheer up. You look so sad. What's the matter?'

'I am a little unhappy, Donald. I thought you would ring me on Sunday or Monday to find out how things went.'

'No, I couldn't do such a thing, Mary. Nothing that goes through the telephone is secret.'

'Then you could have come along.'

'No, I couldn't do such a thing, Mary. I would have aroused loads and loads of suspicion.'

'And supposing I hadn't come here today? What would you have done?'

'I would have sent an envoy. But it can be a very tricky business. Having carried out the job so well, I did not want to ruin it all by doing a stupid thing. You get me?'

'So you know what happened? I carried out your instructions to the letter. You haven't even congratulated me.'

'Congratulations then. But the real congratulations will be coming, and they will be coming in a big way. Remember that before long I will be able to draw on that account in Kampala, being the only signatory, or rather, being the only partner who can now sign a cheque. Your assistance was absolutely essential. You will be well rewarded.'

'How?'

'If I put ten thousand shillings into your account, what would you do with it?'

Jane looked at Donald in disbelief. She just stared at him as if he was made of soapstone.

'Mary, I have also checked about that baby you were telling me about. Remember? What was the mother called? Jane Njeri, or something like that? Why are you looking at me as if I had three eyes, Mary?'

'Because I am not Mary Thama. I gave you a fictitious name to hide my true identity. I had no real reason but I just thought that it would not be proper to reveal my name at a family planning clinic.'

'Wheew! When will beautiful girls learn to be nice and straightforward? And what is your real name, then?'

'I am Jane Njeri. Tell me about my baby. Tell me now. May 15th was the date of birth. Talk, Doctor, talk.'

The doctor was lost in deep thought for a while. He appeared to be uncertain whether to talk or not. But Jane gave him no chance.

'Don't keep quiet, Donald,' she said. 'One good turn deserves another.'

Dr Kalule could no longer keep quiet. This girl had done for him what nobody else would have done. Yes, one good turn deserves another.

'It was a boy. Eight pounds thirteen ounces. Have I talked?'

'Oh Lord, Oh Lord. A boy? And where is my boy now? Talk, Doctor, talk.'

'He was adopted by a well-to-do couple up-country. Religious people, according to the records. The signatory was a bloke called ...'

There was a loud knock at the door. A very loud knock. Much louder than usual. A deep voice came from the other side.

'Open this door, failing which I shall do what I do to doors that don't open.'

Dr Kalule was now trembling. He went and unlocked the door. A tall figure stepped in.

'I am Superintendent Kahiu Kimotho of the Kenya Police ... You are both under arrest.'

Both were handcuffed and led outside. They were taken in different vehicles to different places.

Jane Njeri found herself facing a young and handsome police officer in a small room with a table and two chairs. The officer looked about eighteen, but he could have been twenty or over. Jane had a good idea where she was. Western Police Station, must be.

'You are Jane Njeri, you come from Ihithe in the Nyeri District. You work with a bank. Correct?'

'Correct.'

'Do you want to go to work tomorrow?'

'Yes, I do.'

'Then please do one simple thing. Tell us about Ali Kamau's death. Tell us how Dr Kalule comes into it. You know more than what you told the Superintendent the other day.'

'I will not tell you anything. I don't talk to strangers.'

'I am not a stranger. I am Chief Inspector Kiruhi Mwania of the Kenya Police. I also happened to be a Kenya citizen both outside and inside.'

'That's a rather late introduction. I am Jane Njeri and I have once before helped the police investigate a forgery. Can I have a few words with Number Four? A devil you know is better than ...'

'I am afraid he is off duty. Now, can we get on with the conversation?'

Jane just wouldn't talk. The police officer left and banged the door. He came back after half an hour or so. Jane was taken to the small office on Tom Mboya Street. Number Four was waiting there. He looked tired and overworked. It was now about half past ten at night.

'We meet again, Superintendent. Why all this fuss? Why am I being shunted from one place to another like an unwanted railway wagon?'

'Because one of our best men is dead. I told you about Detective Assistant Yowasi Kizito last Sunday, didn't I? The man commonly known as Ali Kamau.'

Jane now decided to talk. She explained how she came to know the dead man, and how Dr Donald Kalule came into it. She told Kimotho everything, but not about that poison bottle she had.

'That's very useful information, Jane. Very useful information. The Detective Assistant would of course not have told us about his connection with the doctor. He would never have disclosed to us that he had some loot tucked away somewhere in a Kampala bank.' The Superintendent sighed.

'And what do I get for that information?' Jane asked.

'Depends on how you answer my next question. What did you put into his drink?'

Jane was seized by one tiny shock which started somewhere in the region of her kidneys. The little shock travelled upwards and by the time it reached the heart it was one deluge of a shock. Her heart was now beating like the Ashanti drums. She forgot to answer the question.

'You haven't answered my question, Jane. The beer, the glass fragments and some organs of the late Kizito were analysed for poison. I have the report of the analyst. Those people don't guess. Are you with me?'

Jane swallowed once, then swallowed twice. Her most precious secret was no longer a secret.

'I put in a little powder which Dr Kalule gave me,' she said almost in a whisper.

'Do you still have the container?'

'No.'

'Will you sign a statement to this effect?'

'Yes. Haven't I helped you people before?'

'Yes, you have, Jane, and we have not forgotten that.'

'Can I go to work tomorrow, then?'

'Yes, depending on how you answer my next question.'

'Shoot.'

'Why did you do it?'

She explained. It was a bargain. She was to do something for Dr Kalule. In turn, he would tell her about her child. It was a long, pathetic story. Even Superintendent Kimotho, tough as he was, could not help being touched.

'Any more questions, Superintendent?'

'Let me see, let me see.'

'Can I go to work tomorrow?'

'Yes, depending on how you answer my next question.'

'I hope this is your last question, Superintendent.'

'It is.'

'Shoot.'

'Will you at all times be ready to help us in our investigations concerning this case?'

'Yes. Can I go to work tomorrow?'

'Yes. And with my best wishes.'

Superintendent Kimotho now had all the facts. He had authorised the release of the three drunks but they would of course be called to Court to give evidence. The only person in custody was Dr Donald Kalule. He was the only accused.

When the file came up for processing, the State Counsel was unhappy about one or two aspects of the case. He called Superintendent Kimotho, who was the investigating officer for more discussions.

'Superintendent, you have no doubt done a very clean job of this case. We know why Detective Assistant Yowasi Kizito flopped on the table. It ties up with the analyst's report. Cyanide is one of the most poisonous substances known.'

'Yes, it was detected in the beer on the floor, on the glass fragments and in the stomach of our late friend.'

'But then, the official cause of death is declared as cerebral haemorrhage. There will be a long legal battle. We must be ready for it. I suggest we bring in this girl Jane Njeri.'

'There are peculiar circumstances in this case.' The Superintendent explained the whole story about the money in Uganda and all that. 'We haven't seen the end of it yet. I am sure the Uganda Government will want to get to the root of it. We intend to use Jane Njeri for these further investigations. She has been very co-operative on two occasions before and I am sure she is our only hope if these further investigations are to succeed. This is why I have not locked her up yet.'

'Granted. But can we allow a girl to go scot-free after committing a cruel, premeditated murder? After killing one of our most useful investigators? Superintendent, answer me that question.'

Superintendent Kimotho had to go over Jane Njeri's story all over again. About adoption and all that. The State Counsel listened intently. Above all, there would be further investigations and this girl would certainly be useful. The matter involved two sovereign states. Locking Jane Njeri up at this stage might make later investigations virtually impossible. The Superintendent was correct. The State Counsel agreed to process the case against the doctor and to leave the minister's daughter out of it. Maybe she would be more useful outside prison than inside. It was a delicate decision to make. Kimotho was very happy to see things go the way he wanted.

The usual preliminary inquiry was held and the doctor was committed for trial. But a few weaknesses in the case had already come to light. There were long arguments between the prosecution and the defence about the cause of death. Did Ali die of poisoning or did he die of cerebral haemorrhage? But there was no doubt about the doctor's intentions. The doctor's two lawyers defended their client well, but he was found guilty and sentenced to seven years in prison. The doctor was taken to Kabete Jail. Maranga's jail.

7

Back to Ihithe. We missed one or two rather interesting events in that cold place at the bottom of the Aberdares. The cold evening breezes are as cold as ever. The morning frost, especially in January is as frosty as ever. It makes the sweet-potato tops go black. No bananas will grow at Ihithe because of the chill and the frost.

We missed a rumour, a very strong rumour. It went round and round Ihithe for months and months. It must have started at Nairobi, no doubt, and then travelled northwards at rumour speed. This rumour made many people sad. It made Teacher Andrew Karanja sad, very sad indeed. Teacher Andrew Karanja was sad because Bwana Absalom Gacara was sad. Bwana Absalom Gacara was sad because his wife Agatha Waceke would not believe in rumours. She likes being different, this woman. Everybody was talking about the one and only daughter of the one and only Bwana at Ihithe. That she got pregnant. How wicked of her to have got pregnant. That she got a child. That she is now lost in Nairobi. That she is now a prostitute there. That she would never come back home again.

Bwana Absalom tended to believe these rumours. He has always been a believer. His belief was strengthened by the fact that Jane Njeri never came back to Ihithe after she left for Nairobi, when her studies at Tumu Tumu were over. She never wrote home either. Even Gideon Murage had chosen to keep quiet about her. All this was very surprising.

Agatha Waceke did not always see eye to eye with her husband on a lot of things. But she kept her own secrets to herself, and she had quite a few. One of them was her ardent wish that this rumour was true. She really did hope that her only daughter had managed to get herself a child. Not that she would not have liked to see Jane married one day, but some stupid person had told Agatha that girls who are the only children in the family never have babies. Agatha tended to believe this. She kept thinking about it. It became a permanent worry for her.

Agatha did not mind the rumour at all. Getting married is important but having a child is even more important. She had learned this fact the hard way. Girls with children have got married before, some to very good husbands. If her daughter had a baby, that was nothing to worry about. She might still get herself a husband one day.

Perhaps one day she will get to the bottom of this story. Perhaps a day will come when she will see her daughter's child. Patience is no problem with the old folks at Ihithe.

One day Bwana Absalom received a letter. It was from his daughter Jane. It was headed 'Kitui Women's Teachers Training College'. What a blessing. There was a lot of rejoicing that day at Bwana Absalom's home. Jane Njeri was no longer at Nairobi. She was no longer in the city where devils dwell, where evils abound, where the young and the unwary sink into the eternal mud of sin.

The good news was spread all over Ihithe. Bwana Absalom

preached to all and sundry that the Lord God of Israel has never let anybody down and never will.

True, because when Jane Njeri left, the Lord brought in this new child. This lovely boy, this pleasure of the home. This boy who was adopted. We missed his baptism, which was no small occasion. He was baptised Joshua Abednego. These two names just popped off Bwana Absalom's head. The surname is traditional, there was no guesswork here. It had to be the name of the father of the Bwana, whose name is Mathai. So the little boy is called Joshua Abednego Mathai.

Joshua grew up to be a very playful boy, more playful than the other boys of his age. He grew up well protected from hunger and disease. He was protected from cold, from loneliness, from unbelief. He cherished and loved his parents, he obeyed their commands and respected their steady way of life. There was discipline, but firm, reasonable discipline.

Oh, we missed Joshua's first day at school as well. That was recent, very recent indeed. The headmaster at Ihithe was there. Teacher Andrew Karanja was there to organise things generally and to give a little welcoming speech. Bwana Absalom's son is not like the other sons.

Teacher Andrew Karanja had always been the *de facto* headmaster at Ihithe. Without him, this place would collapse. The whole of Ihithe knew it, and they accepted it. One Education Officer at Nyeri wanted to transfer Teacher Andrew Karanja to another school. A big delegation was sent to Nyeri from Ihithe. The chief was there, so too were all the sub-chiefs together with the local KANU chairman. They told this officer a few things which have never been revealed. And the result? The Education Officer was transferred from Nyeri to Moyale. Poor fellow.

We also missed this wedding that was to be. But the locals didn't, not all of them. Definitely not at Maranga's home. They wetted themselves thoroughly with the native hooch. Some used horns, others used cups. The food brought in by the women was neglected. But not the roast meat. The men ate the ribs, the women were given the backbone. You know the backbone, the thing that has lots of small bones sticking out so that you cannot get at the meat? That's what the women got. If anybody tells you that they will soon be women's-libbing up at Ihithe, don't catch pneumonia. The groundwork has already been laid, and in style.

The road from Nyeri to Ihithe was not quite so good, not those days. It was full of gullies and potholes. In places it was always wet. Many people thought that the wedding couple might have got bogged down. Or their cars might have failed to climb the Ihithe hills. These hills are very steep. You engaged the first gear and the car coughs out half-way up the hill. Your passengers come out, you engage the first gear again, and the car coughs out after running five yards. Maybe this is what happened. Maybe they are still pushing those cars. But the drinking went on regardless.

It was on the following day that most folks came to know that Lewis Maranga and his bride had had to cancel their wedding at the eleventh hour. Bwana Absalom came to the wedding home. He offered an explanation. First, he said, Lewis Maranga should not have become a clerk. All clerks end up in prison because they steal money. He should have become a teacher. Secondly, he should not have become a clerk with a beer company. All beer drinkers will go to hell because the Bible says so. Thirdly, he should not have got married to a girl without the approval of his parents. This is against the Fourth Commandment. Bwana Absalom had answers to everything.

Well, well, let's go back to jail, Kabete Jail to be precise. We can afford to miss what's going on at Ihithe because there is nothing very much going on there, but we can't afford to miss what's going on at Kabete Jail.

Both Kalule and Maranga were model prisoners. They had to be. They knew only too well that if they got marks for good behaviour, they stood a good chance of having their sentences reduced by one or two years.

One problem the science of penology does not appear to have solved is how to discriminate between a habitual criminal and an

142

intelligent, educated man of means who finds himself at logger-heads with the law. Kalule and Maranga are good examples. These two people had broken the law. Both of them had committed serious crimes. But then, the mental agony which they went through as a result of finding themselves in jail is not quite what a habitual criminal would go through.

Not quite. To a jailbird, like one bloke in this very same prison called Menja, jail can be fun. To him, life has a distorted image, a funny unreal reality of its own, and a jail is just one of those funny establishments in society for people who do not do what the majority of humans do. A jail is like a hospital where you have to go to when you are sick and the others are not.

Menja, for example, would be very sad indeed if he wasn't in jail every Christmas. He admitted it, he confessed it, he liked Christmas in jail. It is the only place where he would be fed, clothed and housed, not to mention the entertainment that the prisoners get to commemorate the birth of Christ.

But for Kalule and Maranga, things were different. It was mental agony to begin with, the type of agony that is known to induce a complete personality change. Kalule and Maranga were definitely suffering more than a person like Menja was. But not for long.

Take Donald Kalule, for example. He was made the orderly in charge of the prison dispensary after two and a half years in jail. For a medical consultant, this is a very simple job. He could have treated all those minor colds, sores, fevers and tummyaches with his eyes closed.

It was a good, useful way of passing his time in jail. Warder Wambua would open up the dispensary in the morning. Kalule would clean up the place and get out syringes, swabs, and bandages ready to see the sick. And there were many of them every day. A prisoner who complains of being sick has to be attended to. You can't ignore him. He may drop dead on you. You may have to answer a lot of questions. Prison Warders do not like being subjected to inquiries, inquests and inquisitions just because they did not take a complaining prisoner to the dispensary, especially if there was one just around the corner.

Kalule, who was now called simply Kalule and not Dr Kalule, was only answerable to the prison doctor on medical matters. The prison doctor used to come in in the morning. His was a part-time job. Kalule would have disposed of all the minor cases but the more difficult ones would wait for him. It was only the prison doctor who could issue drugs, make prescriptions or recommend that a patient be taken to the Kenyatta National Hospital. But not always. If the prisoner became sick all of a sudden and the prison doctor could not be contacted easily, Kalule would advise Warder Wambua what to do. Warder Wambua would not want to hear that a prisoner had collapsed and died simply because Kalule was not consulted. Not when there were so many vehicles around to take the sick to Kenyatta. And remember, nobody wants inquiries, inquests and inquisitions.

Kalule had a nice time in jail, let me tell you. He was superior to the other prisoners, especially with that white coat on and the stethoscope hanging on his neck. Many prisoners refused to believe that this man was a prisoner himself.

Kalule's favourite game was talking to his patients about their crimes. The urge to know what those people had done to deserve isolation from society was almost pathological in him. He could hardly go to sleep if during the day he had not heard a good story or two. He enjoyed listening as he tied a bandage or listened to the heartbeat. If the story was really good, he would prolong the treatment so as to give the prisoner a chance to tell all without undue hurry.

Warder Wambua was always around, of course. But he was not the type that liked to see ulcers being dressed or syringe needles being sunk into people's behinds. He was allergic to this kind of thing. He was quite contented to watch his prisoners from a safe distance. The only occasions he would go inside the dispensary were when he wanted an aspirin or two, especially after the weekends.

Here is a conversation between Kalule and one of his patients who had come to have his ulcer dressed.

'What are you in for? A young and vigorous man like you should not be here.'

'I am young and vigorous, that's why.'

'This country needs people who are young and vigorous. We require productive human resources. A country of lazy people cannot go ahead and our incessant efforts to raise the standards of our people will be nullified. Oh, I digress. What did you say you are in for?'

'Rape. That's what.'

'I see. You mean you had what they call carnal knowledge of a woman without her knowledge and consent?'

'No, definitely not. I had her full knowledge and consent. If anybody was unwilling to do it, it was me. And I got locked up, she didn't.' Kalule could hardly believe this. It sounded like a tall story.

'Say that again? And in case nobody has told you, I went to school. I am not the type that you live with out there. Do you get me? You know the type that you can tell anything to and they will believe it? I am not that type.'

'I will tell you the whole story, but I will leave out the non-sensical bits.'

'No, holy Lord, no. Those are the bits that I want to hear,' Kalule says.

'Well, one day we went to a drinking party. My home is up in Mbere at a place called Kanyuanjui. In Mbere when people drink, they drink. They don't spoil it by eating maize and beans and things like that in between.'

'Yes, or bananas for that matter. Go on.'

'In the evening, everybody went home but I couldn't. I was very drunk. I could hardly walk. I flopped down on the sack next to the fireplace in the house and slept there.'

'Certainly. Good African socialism. Your home is my home and my home is mine too. Who says we want all these new changes?' Kalule was enjoying himself.

'Not me, I assure you. So I sleep on this sack, snoring like a kangaroo with asthma.'

'You don't go to jail for that.'

'But there is one thing I do not know. This sack is the bed of the daughter of the woman who made the beer. This girl may have taken a little beer herself, I don't know. She comes and sleeps next to me. Maybe she thinks that I will quit her bed. But not me. I am not a coward. Run away because of a woman? Me?'

'Not only you, even me. I wouldn't run away from a girl for anything.'

'At night I wake up. The girl is still there. Her mother does not appear to have taught this girl very good manners. Either that, or else she thought I was a mule.'

'Of course you are not a mule. You have two legs and not four.'

'You have good eyesight, I must say. But what was worrying me was the fact that this girl had no objection.'

'Why should she? And you?'

'I was quite reluctant at first. You know how things are with a lot of drink? But then I thought I better oblige.'

'Like a good Samaritan, eh?'

'Yes. But what happens the following morning? The girl tells the whole story to her mother, and in great detail too. Me, I had forgotten all about it, but not this girl. Women are terrific when it comes to remembering some things.'

'They remember them for life, let me tell you. They really do.'

'And the way she told it. She looked extremely amused. But her mummy was not so amused. She went and told the chief who was also not so amused either. He sent one of his guards who called the police. The girl was taken all the way to Embu Hospital for examination. I was arrested that same day.'

'And then? Make it short because the next patient appears to have a very bad cough.'

'I was taken to Court. This Magistrate asked me to describe in detail what happened. He wanted the truth. He was really enjoying himself, this man. Some of his questions were searching, very searching indeed.'

'So what happened? What was the sentence?'

'I got five years and six strokes.'

'For what?'

'For defiling a girl under sixteen years. The Magistrate said that I should have waited for a year because this girl was only fifteen.'

'How did he know that she was only fifteen?'

'A doctor counted her teeth or something. If you asked me, I would have said that she was at least eighteen. Doctors can also go wrong, you know.'

'Why would you have said that she was at least eighteen?'

'Not only did she have a lot of teeth, she was a perfect lady in every respect.'

'Don't worry brother, don't worry. That is what is called a technical offence.'

'True, but they didn't send me to a technical jail. This one is real. And those canes. They were not technical, I assure you. On top of that, my life will never be the same again.'

' 'Bye for now. Your ulcer will heal before they release you. Maybe the girl is still waiting for you and, believe me, you will be in very good shape when you go back home. Besides, she is bound to be well over sixteen when you get back.'

The next patient had a rather bad cough. He came up and sat on a stool.

'Don't worry about the cough, brother. I'll take your temperature and listen to your heartbeat. I'll give you medicine and if the cough still persists, I shall ask the prison doctor to see you. How long have you been here?'

'Two years and six months.'

'Just like me. What made you come here?'

'Nothing very much. Somebody fabricated a story about forging cheques and that sort of thing. If you have friends who work with the Kenya Beer Agencies, ask them to be very careful. If those people don't like you, they will get rid of you in a very nasty way.'

'I understand. Somebody must have got jealous of your money. If you don't have money, you get into trouble. If you sweat hard and get it, you still get into trouble. This is a strange world. Did they confiscate your money?'

'No, and this is the proof that the whole thing was a fabrication. They told me that I was guilty of stealing the money. But they wouldn't touch it. It's my own money and they know it. But it is now rather useless because I cannot get at it.'

Strange. Because Doctor Kalule himself had a lot of useless money lying in a bank in Kampala. Prisoners can share the same problems without realising it.

'Your name is Maranga? How do you pronounce that?'

'Just the way it is written, Ma-ra-nga. My first name is Lewis.'

'I am Donald Kalule. I think we should talk to each other more often. I guess you were at school for a long time?'

'Yes. Up to School Certificate. I never in my whole life thought that I would ever see the inside of a jail. But there it is. And you?'

'I never dreamed of it either. Not after going up to degree level and all that. Do you know of any other prisoner here who has a good education like us?'

'No, Kalule. We must be the only two prisoners here with some education. I think we are rather unlucky, don't you think so? Imagine going through a life like this with loads of money lying in the bank. Just imagine that.'

Dr Kalule did not need to imagine anything. He had already gone through the torture and the misery of being locked up. But all things come to an end some time. He vowed to himself to see this prisoner Maranga more often. They had a number of problems in common. Maybe there is a solution to some of them.

'You and I are the brains in this prison. Maybe we can use our brains to good effect. Keep using yours and I will keep using mine. And make sure you come here tomorrow, won't you?'

'So long as I am still coughing, I will definitely turn up.'

'Even if the cough disappears, think of something else. Cheerio.'

The next patient did not look very good. He appeared to have had extensive injuries some time in the past. He had come for regular checking.

'What happened?' Kalule asked.

'I broke my limbs when I was trying to escape.'

'To escape? You must be a very daring person.'

'I have always told myself that I can do what anybody else can do. Some friends of mine had escaped two weeks before. I was feeling lonely and so I decided to have a go. I persuaded a few other prisoners to come along with me.'

'How? You don't look like the sort of person who would break records in high jump. Or was it pole vault?'

'No. Jumping is a little old-fashioned these days.'

'What is the modern method?'

'Violence. Violence will never get out of date.'

The man explained in great detail how they did it. It was an interesting story to listen to. Kalule kept nodding his head as this prisoner talked.

'Then what happened?'

'Once we were outside, we didn't know what to do with ourselves. We had no previous plan as to what we would do. We just ran around like a bunch of frightened rabbits. We also began feeling rather lonely, out there. No friends, nobody to talk to, nothing. After two days we were all collected and brought back here.'

'With two or three years on top of the old sentence?'

'No, strangely, no. We were never taken to Court. I suppose the prison authorities did not want the escape story to come out.'

'And your name? Did you tell me your name?'

'Menja. Just call me Menja. And you?'

'Kalule. You will turn up tomorrow, won't you? It will be my turn to tell you a story, right?'

That night, Donald Kalule slept very little. A lot of ideas kept going through his head. The next day the patients were back. He was interested in two patients only. Lewis Maranga was one. Menja was the other.

'Maranga, how do you feel?'

'Fine, thank you. And you?'

'Not quite so good, I am afraid. With a chequebook lying at home and plenty of money in the bank, I can assure you that I don't feel quite so good. I have money in Nairobi and I have money in Kampala, yet I am rotting in a stinking jail. Did you tell me that you are feeling good?'

'No. I have changed my mind. I am not feeling quite so good either.'

'Why?'

'Because I have a chequebook locked up in a box at Makadara. I have a lot of money lying idle in a bank. Just like you, Kalule.'

'Let's change the topic, Maranga. How many big jails do you know?'

'This one, Kabete. I think I know other big ones but their names escape me.'

'Ever heard of San Quentin?'

'Oh yes, San Quentin.'

'Ever heard of Wormwood Scrubs?'

'Oh yes, Wormwood Scrubs.'

'And what have all these places got in common apart from being jails and having prisoners inside them?'

'That's a difficult one, Kalule. It sounds like a quiz.'

'No, Maranga, it isn't. The answer is simple. Prisoners have escaped from these jails, every one of them. Call them maximum security prisons if you want, but it makes no difference. Are you with me?'

'Yes. What are you up to, Kalule?'

'If you want to get to your chequebook and withdraw some money the day after tomorrow, I will show you how.'

'How? I would do anything to get out of here.'

Donald Kalule explained his plan to Lewis Maranga. It was a simple plan. Donald Kalule had not lost his sleep for nothing.

But Kalule had one little worry. This prisoner Maranga did not appear to be the courageous type. However, he was eager to co-operate and that is what mattered.

Kalule gave the same instructions to Menja. He was very happy with Menja's response. This was a prisoner who would do anything. Menja was ready to do anything in order to make Kalule's plan a complete success.

The following day was like any other day at Kabete Jail. Groups of prisoners went about their daily routine as usual. Some, like Menja, went to the workshops, while others, like Maranga, went to the prison gardens. Kalule went to his dispensary as usual.

Warder Wambua watched the patients with the eye of an eagle. They were brought into the dispensary by the other warders. During treatment, they were in his charge. They were his responsibility until they got out of the dispensary door.

But Warder Wambua did not really cherish the idea of watching Kalule do whatever he did to human beings from too close a range. He hardly entered the dispensary. The only time he did was when the prison doctor turned up at eleven o'clock. Then he would go in and chat with him. He would also take down the particulars of those patients whose condition was serious enough to warrant their being taken to the Kenyatta National Hospital. He would then arrange for transport and have them sent there for treatment.

The prison doctor came at eleven o'clock as usual on this particular day.

'Morning, Wambua. How are your prisoners getting on?'

'Pretty fine, Doctor. We have very good prisoners here.'

'Good. And you, Kalule? Anything for me today?'

'No, no serious cases. But I require some drugs. We should keep them handy just in case something happens.'

The doctor was given a list of drugs. He issued them from the dispensary store and was just about to go when Kalule opened his mouth to talk.

'Doctor, there is one thing I want to know. What would you recommend I should do if I were to be confronted with a rather serious case in the middle of the night?'

'Such as what, Kalule?'

'Such as tetanus or food poisoning?'

'Oh, there is just one thing to do if that happens. Get the patient taken to Kenyatta National Hospital as soon as practicable. By all means don't wait. Better give me a ring so that we all meet at the hospital.'

'Quite true, Doctor,' Warder Wambua added. 'We don't want patients to drop dead on us, do we?

'No Wambua,' the doctor added. 'Nobody wants inquiries, inquests and inquisitions. Not us.'

At nine o'clock that evening, Warder Wambua had not yet retired to bed. The duty officer knocked on his door and told him that there was a prisoner who was not feeling well.

'Which one?'

'Lewis Maranga. He also appears to have cut himself rather badly on his big toe during the day.'

'Cut himself where?'

'On the big toe.

'Is it bandaged?'

'Yes.'

'Then ask him to go back to bed until tomorrow morning.'

The duty officer went away, then came back in a few minutes.

'I think this prisoner is really sick. He says that he was not treated. He just tied himself with an old bandage. That toe is full of mud and blood and that sort of thing.'

'What a damned fool! Why didn't he ask to be taken to the dispensary?'

'And what's more, there is another prisoner who is complaining of a terrible stomach ache. That fellow called Menja, do you remember him?'

'O.K., O.K. Go and call Kalule at once. Tell him to wait at the dispensary. Take the two sick prisoners there as well. Tell them I am coming. But be careful of this fellow Menja. You know his history, don't you?'

Warder Wambua is a typical prison guard. He is a large man with a wide face and he moves in slow motion. Above all, he carries a tremendous bunch of keys. There is a long story about this bunch of keys. It is the most important bunch of keys in the whole prison, but that's another story. It normally took him about five minutes to sort out the dispensary key during the day. Now that it was night, it took him twice as long. The sick prisoners were with him.

'Get in, everybody, get in,' he said after the dispensary was open. 'I will remain outside and take a sniff of fresh air.'

Kalule went about his job in the right manner. He talked to his patients rather loudly. Warder Wambua could not help hearing what was going on inside the dispensary. This was part of the plan.

'When did you cut this toe?'

'Maybe about three o'clock or so.'

'And why didn't you report to me at once?'

'I didn't think it was that serious.'

'I see that you have got a lot of mud on it.'

'We were out in the gardens. How can you avoid soil and mud when you are digging?'

'O.K. I'll fix it.' Which he did.

He now moved to the next patient. Menja was enjoying himself thoroughly. This fellow is a habitual criminal, a nut, a jailbird, the sort of fellow who would do anything. He could chop a man's head off and still go on laughing or break into any house in the small hours of the morning without having to read any directions. And of course people like these have no conscience. They only pretend to change when it is good for them, or when they want something, such as to be released quickly.

Menja is a man of action, a criminal who will stop at nothing. All he requires is support from somewhere, some sort of a pillar on which to lean. There was Kalule in this particular case. He was the brains. Menja was ready to supply the hands. He had done it many a time before.

Kalule examined Menja very thoroughly. But Warder Wambua was now wondering why Lewis Maranga had not been released.

'Kalule, can Maranga go back to his cell?'

'No, this kid is sick, very sick. He has early symptoms of tetanus. That soil on his cut toe did not do him any good.'

'Gracious. What do we do? Can I call the prison doctor?'

'No use. We have no tetanus antitoxin here or anything like that. Why not tell him to come up to Kenyatta National Hospital and find us there? At any rate, I doubt whether the doctor will be at home at this time.'

'Gracious. Can the other prisoner be escorted back? Menja, I mean?'

'Tonight is not a good night for you and me, Warder Wambua. It looks as if we are going to have to do without some sleep. Our friend Menja has an acute stomach ache. It looks like food poisoning to me. Don't ask me where he got it from, I don't know. But people have died in as little as eight hours from food poisoning.'

'Oh, I see! In that case we shall have to go to Kenyatta National Hospital. Be ready. I shall telephone the doctor and ask him to meet us at the hospital.'

Turning to the duty officer, he said, 'I want one van and a driver here in five minutes.' Which was done.

Maranga and Menja were handcuffed for the journey. Kalule was too important a person to be handcuffed. What if somebody fainted on the way? He might die before the handcuffs were removed.

Kalule prepared his medical kit and was ready in no time. By a quarter to ten that night, the group was on the way to the hospital. The driver was alone in front. Warder Wambua and the three prisoners were in the back. These prison vans are the type in which the people at the back cannot communicate with the driver. The back compartment was fully enclosed in thick, strong wire gauze. The back door was bolted and padlocked from the inside.

As soon as they were outside the prison gates, Kalule engaged Warder Wambua in a conversation on the dangers of tetanus.

Then he talked about food poisoning and how one dirty plate could finish a man's life. Menja's life, for example. The two prisoners kept bending themselves over with pain. They groaned and moaned. It was part of the plan.

Then Kalule chose a good moment and a good location. It had to be a rather lonely part of the road. He suggested that Menja could do with a little medicine to keep him comfortable. He put his hand into his medical kit and pulled out a plastic bottle which contained a colourless liquid. He slowly screwed out the cap. Then Kalule went to work like lightning. He splashed the liquid into Warder Wambua's eyes, nose and mouth. Then he poured the rest of the liquid on top of the Warder's head. It was like a crude kind of baptism. Warder Wambua gasped once or twice then flopped down on the vehicle floor.

Menja was enjoying the drama tremendously. He now rose up and was about to kick Warder Wambua on the head as he lay down. But Kalule objected.

'Keep away, Menja. That liquid is dangerous.'

It was. Chloroform is not what everybody takes for their tea. It puts people to sleep whether they like it or not. Kalule's dose was a little on the high side, and, all things considered, Warder Wambua will be sleeping maybe until morning. If he has a strong constitution, he will wake up in the end. If anybody throws chloroform on you, you better call him a nasty word in a hurry because if you are slow about it you will find yourself dozing off before saying a thing.

Maranga looked a bit overawed by all this. He is definitely not the violent type. He went on staring at Warder Wambua. He opened his mouth when the Warder attempted to open his eyes. He thought that the poor fellow was dying. He had never seen anybody dying before and he did not want to see it for the first time.

'He won't die,' Kalule assured him, 'but he will have to allow us to do what we want to do. He will be asleep until tomorrow.'

Menja was not quite happy to be left out. 'Can I kick him on the head, Kalule? Or shall we let you take all the honours by yourself?'

'You better not, Menja. If you bash him on the head, he may never wake up again.'

'Do you want him to wake up? Then why all this fuss?'

Menja takes a long time to understand. Inside his head, only two words have any meaning. Violence, that's one. Death, that's the other.

Kalule was going through the Warder's pockets within no time. He pulled out the huge bunch of keys. Within seconds, Maranga and Menja had no handcuffs on them. He also unlocked the back door of the van.

You should have seen Menja's smile when he saw his shackles being unlocked. The handcuffs were thrown into a corner of the van.

The driver carried on regardless. He did not know what was going on in the back. These prison vehicles have a nasty habit of rattling rather loudly for no particular reason. This, together with the fact that the driver was in his own compartment, made it even more difficult for him to know what was going on in the back.

Next, Kalule unlocked the back door. Menja now went into action. He pushed out the big spare tyre which was lying in the van towards the door. Then he let it fall out, flat on its side. It made a great thumping noise as it fell on the road.

Menja now shouted, 'Warder Wambua has fallen out! Warder Wambua has fallen out!' The others joined in the singing. The chorus was repeated again and again. It was like an impromptu choir, with Menja doing the conducting. But the noise was excessive, so excessive that even the driver could hear it in his ivory tower. He lowered the window and looked back. The prisoners were definitely alarmed at something. He pulled to the side of the road and applied his brakes.

Menja did not wait for the van to stop. He snatched Kalule's medical kit and pulled out another plastic container which had the good liquid inside. There was nothing else in that kit. Just bottles and bottles of chloroform.

'Be careful, Menja,' Kalule warned him. 'That liquid is dangerous.'

'Forget it, Kalule. I will do it the way you did.' Menja may be slow to learn, but he is certainly quick to act.

The three prisoners now jumped out of the vehicle. Menja ran towards the driver's compartment. He unscrewed the cap and poured the liquid all over the driver's head and face. He even tried to make him drink a little of it. Then he watched him. The driver did not go to sleep quickly. So Menja punched him on the nose. It all happened so fast that the poor driver had no chance. Ultimately he slumped on his seat and went to sleep.

Menja was feeling very good just now. He raised his hands up to signify that the battle was over.

Kalule looked at both Menja and Maranga. There was no doubt which of them was enjoying the situation. Menja was the person to give the next order to.

'Run back, Menja, to the tyre that we dropped. Roll it out of the road and into the bush. We don't want the next police patrol car to come tumbling into an obstacle like that. Somebody may want to find out what's the story behind that tyre.'

Menja ran back and did his job. All the way along, he was in full admiration of this liquid that Kalule had. Then he ran back to the van.

'Have you got any more of that liquid, Kalule?'

'What for, Menja?'

'We may need it.'

'What for?'

'Look at yourself, Kalule, look at Maranga, look at me. These clothes. They are only fit for the prison. And that's where we do not want to go back to, Kalule. Can we splash the liquid on the next three gentlemen to come along? The next three well-dressed gentlemen?'

'No, Menja. The warder and the driver are not naked, are they?

157

Remove their clothes. We could do with those clothes. They are more useful to us than three woollen Saville Row suits. Maranga, you better help Menja. Those boys are rather heavy and they may require a little turning over to get their clothes off. But be careful not to breathe that liquid too much. If you feel dizzy, jump out of the vehicle. I will keep watch. If I whistle with my lips, you better disappear into the bush and stay there. If you find an empty porcupine hole, you better get into it even if the porcupine puts up some resistance.'

Maranga did not like the job of handling those warm bodies and removing their clothes. They were breathing rather heavily and they were sweating like hell. At last, their uniforms were off.

'Has anybody seen us, chief?' Menja asked. 'We have their uniforms. How do we share them out?'

'Can't leave our two friends with their underclothes only. Not at this time of the night. It's against medical ethics. They may die of pneumonia or something. Get your clothes off and give them to the warder. Maranga will keep his prison clothes on. I will give mine to the driver. Can we do this in ten minutes or so?' It was done.

The warder and the driver were now dressed in prison clothes. Kalule put on the driver's uniform and Menja put on Warder Wambua's uniform. It was too big for him but this did not matter.

'Good,' Kalule said. 'Now comes the most difficult part of the operation. The driver must be taken to the back of the van. It's a shame that those two buddies should have started off the journey separated like that. If they had consulted me, they would not have done it that way.'

The driver was not a light fellow. But it was no problem slumping him into the back. Kalule was now feeling great.

'Now, gentlemen,' he said, 'take your positions. Maranga, you are still a prisoner, don't forget that. You will go to the back and stay there with your sleepy friends.'

Maranga obeyed the order the way a humble schoolboy runs when the headmaster asks him to run.

Kalule followed him into the back of the vehicle. He handcuffed the two snoring gentlemen.

'There are no handcuffs for you, Maranga, but if we come across any danger, I want you to lie down just like these other two. But you must lie on your hands so that nobody can see that you have no handcuffs on you. Right?'

'Right. What's the next step, Kalule? I thought that we were going to escape from prison. But you are making the show much too elaborate. Far too elaborate for me. Where do we go to from here? I am still thinking of that chequebook lying in a box at Makadara. See that I get to it some time.'

'Don't worry, Maranga. I thought that the two of us were the only brains in prison. I regret to say that I have now changed my mind.'

'Because of?'

'Menja. We are three brains, not two. He is a fine lad. As fine a lad as any that walks on two legs.' True, because some criminals are very intelligent human beings.

'Or wields a hammer on a man's head or drinks his blood,' Maranga snarled. 'Get going with your plans. But if you make them too complicated, we will run straight into the hands of the police or something. But perhaps I'd better shut up.'

'Quite. I didn't lose my sleep last night for nothing. But we must be going. Just bolt the back door. I will keep my medical kit. I hope we won't need it again, but who knows? Come on, Menja. You will accompany me in front.'

Menja sat on the passenger's seat. Kalule tried the ignition and shifted the gear lever to and fro.

'It's different from a Peugeot, I assure you. But we shall see how we get along.'

Then engine started with no problems. Kalule engaged the reverse gear.

'I will go back, Menja. You will tell me where that tyre is. It's crazy going on a journey without a spare tyre.'

He reversed the van to where the tyre was. They put it into the back of the van and got going. They would have to go along Kabete Road and into Westlands. From there it was anybody's guess where Kalule would drive the van to.

Maranga's heart was now thumping inside his chest like the Ashanti drums. Not only did he feel rather lonely with those two unconscious prison officers next to him, he was wondering whether the whole idea was not kind of crazy. Having disabled the warder and his driver, was it really necessary to pinch the prison vehicle as well?

Maranga's fears were increased by the fact that Kalule did not appear to be quite familiar with this van. He would sometimes drive too much to the left and then go too far to the right like somebody who was having trouble with the steering wheel. Or somebody who was drunk.

You can therefore imagine what Maranga felt inside him when he saw a little red notice saying, 'Police Check Ahead'. He wanted to scream. He began sweating. He remembered what he had told Kalule. They would run straight into the hands of the police. And that was exactly where they were heading for. But he also remembered what he had been asked to do should they get into trouble. To lie low and be dead. Which he did.

When Kalule saw the red little sign, a quick wave of confusion ran through him. Reversing was out of the question. There were cars in front and cars behind. There was only one thing to do. Put on an innocent face, keep as calm as possible, keep the car on the road and drive on regardless. After all, he was dressed like a prison driver. Menja was in the official uniform of a prison warder and there were three prisoners at the back, all in clean prison uniform.

He drove the vehicle past the red notice and came to the main checkpoint. Huge wooden boards with great long nails sticking out of them were all over the road. They were placed in such a way that one had to drive very carefully to pass them. One had to pass the first one on the left, and the next one on the right, and so on to the end.

This meant driving slowly, making many sharp esses. But when the car is strange to you, and you are a frightened, sweating prisoner escaping from jail, there is something extra that frightens you apart from the esses. Not lack of confidence, because Kalule had plenty of that. Not lack of courage, or guts, or nerves of steel, because all that was not lacking. But there was that other thing which made Kalule's hands shake a little. One could call it confrontation with reality. It is the most frightening of all confrontations, especially if the reality cannot be dreamed away.

But Menja was not affected. When confronted with reality like this, Menja simply switches his thinking mechanism off. He gets ready to act according to the dictates of his subconscious, according to a pre-set formula which is not fabricated on the spot. He just talks or acts like a violent machine.

'Kalule,' Menja said, 'be careful and drive well. If anything nasty happens, I know where your medical kit is.'

'Shut up, you idiot, and let me handle this. Try not to get into it, please.'

'Kalule, I am burning to get into it nice and proper. Tonight I will kill at least five people. Five is not a large number, you know.'

Kalule gave up talking. They had come up to the checkpoint proper. Inspector Joram approached them cautiously. He had a casual look at the vehicle and then at the driver.

'I think I have seen you before, driver?' he said.

'Yes, I am Wanyama. Remember me?'

'How is Kabete? Any prisoners escaped of late?'

'No. They can't. But they get sick far too often. I am on the way to the hospital. I am in a bit of a rush for obvious reasons.' Inspector Joram let them go.

Kalule got going. He passed the first board on the left, then the next on the right, and so on till he came up to the last one. He was just about to pass it when he went too far to the left and partly got into the ditch. He revved up the engine and got himself out. Then he headed straight for Uhuru Highway.

One constable became suspicious of Kalule's driving. He thought he should talk. But he had his doubts. The senior officers would laugh at him. He himself was not quite certain whether his suspicion was worth a dime. But he could not keep quiet. He came up with a nice trick. He chose to talk to himself.

'The driver of that prison van is probably drunk,' he said aloud.

'Constable Peter,' somebody called, 'do you really think so? Why?' This was Chief Inspector Noel Kimamo, the officer in charge of this patrol.

'He got into the ditch at the last board, sir. I have also been watching him right from the beginning. His driving is a little suspicious. But perhaps this is not important.'

'What do you mean, it is not important? Supposing he is drunk, Constable. A uniformed prison driver drunk. And supposing we let him through. And supposing he caused an accident. We would have to answer a lot of questions, wouldn't we? Call Inspector Joram. He is the one who talked to that driver.'

Inspector Joram was called. He came in a hurry because he knew that Chief Inspector Kimamo does not call somebody for nothing.

'Inspector, were you close enough to this prison driver? Did he smell of alcohol?'

'I would say no, but I am not quite sure. I was not suspicious of anything wrong with him. Besides, prison drivers are the very pinnacle of perfection when it comes to handling mechanically driven vehicles.'

'Well, this one wasn't. He got into the ditch at that end. We better make sure. Inspector, you stay here. If I don't come back soon, call the operation off. Constable, come with me. They are heading for the hospital and that is where we shall also head for.'

They got into a patrol car and got going. They caught up with the van in no time at a point just before coming to the P.C.'s office. Chief Inspector Kimamo chose to conduct the conversation this time.

'Sorry to stop you again, but we suspected that one of your tyres does not have enough pressure and you should be careful not to go too fast. How many people have you got in the back?'

'Three. One is very sick and the other two are dying.'

Chief Inspector Noel Kimamo was not interested in the sick and the dying. He was more interested in the driver. He was now certain that the driver had no alcohol in him but he was still not happy. Good policemen have a sixth sense which tells them when there is something wrong somewhere, even if it cannot be pinpointed in exact terms. But when you are dealing with a prison driver, it is difficult to know how to go about the difficult task of investigating while still remaining neutral and friendly. But Chief Inspector Kimano is no fool in his job.

'Tell me, are these cases serious?'

'Very. Two especially are really bad, as I have already told you.'

'And the prison doctor?'

'He is at Kenyatta. We arranged to meet him there.'

'Sorry for the inconvenience. I am sure your prisoners will get well. But remember not to go too fast. Cheerio.'

Chief Inspector Kimamo went straight to the hospital. The doctor's car was there. The doctor himself was walking to and fro at the hospital's main door.

'Hello, Doctor. Three prison patients are on their way here. I have just passed them. They should be here any minute now.'

'Goodness gracious. It is now eleven o'clock. They rang me at about nine o'clock. It should not take two hours to travel from Kabete Jail to here. I feel like resigning this prison job and concentrating on my private practice.'

'Don't worry, Doctor. They should be here any minute now. I would say five minutes. I will stay with you until they come.'

Quite. The Chief Inspector was still suspicious of something. That's why he chose to wait until the prison van arrived. So he stayed with the doctor.

Five minutes passed. Ten minutes, twenty, half an hour,

forty-five minutes, still no prison van. One hour passed, still no prison van came.

'Doctor, you can go home and have some sleep.'

'And you, Chief Inspector?'

'I want that prison van with all those in it, dead or alive.'

8

Donald Kalule drove the van slowly. That is what Chief Inspector Noel Kimamo asked him to do. There is a proverb which says that too much hurry has no blessing. There is also another proverb which says that it is the early bird that catches the worm. Pity, because it also means that it is the early worm that gets caught. Why people still believe in proverbs, I don't know.

The van chugged its way up to Kenyatta Avenue, and into Ngong Road. Before long, it was standing outside Dr Kalule's old home.

The three escaped prisoners got out. They rushed to the servants' quarters. Dr Kalule's old servant was still there. He did not like being woken up at midnight. But he could not mistake the voice of the caller.

'Oh, Doctor, oh, Doctor, is it you?' he exclaimed.

'Yes, it's me. I got released from jail today. I want to do a few things in a hurry. Open the house, quick.'

Kalule went into his old house and stuffed a lot of clothes and things into one box. He was particularly careful to take his cheque-books. He had a lot of clothes, this man. Enough for everybody around.

He changed into his favourite suit. Then he chose some clothes for Menja. Menja looked very smart in one of Kalule's old suits. Maranga also wore one of Kalule's old suits.

'Menja, take this box into the van. We must hurry. The sleeping dogs in the van may wake up any time now.'

Menja took the box away. Kalule took this opportunity to have a last conversation with his servant.

'What happened to the car?'

'The garage people took it away. They told me that they would credit its value to your bank account.'

'Good. But you must not tell anybody that I was here. After we are gone, lock the place up exactly as it was. If anybody asks you whether I have been here, tell them that I am still in jail. Do you get me?'

The story did not make sense but Kalule's servant did not ask any questions. Kalule wrote out a cheque and gave it to him.

'Deposit that tomorrow in your own account. It is enough to keep you going for quite some time. Cheerio.'

Maranga now joined his colleagues in front and the van headed for Makadara. This was a dangerous journey because they would have to traverse a good deal of the town centre. But luck was on their side. Chief Inspector Noel Kimamo was still at the hospital. He was still waiting for the prison van.

Kalule parked the van a good distance from the Makadara block where Maranga used to live. Maranga left quietly and went and knocked at the door. He was almost dying with nostalgia.

'Bethwell, Bethwell, Lewis here. Lewis Maranga. Please open.'

The baby woke up and cried. Mrs Mbarathi had two children already. Remember Grace Wangare who used to work for Gideon Murage?

There was a good deal of commotion, excitement and general confusion. When Bethwell saw Maranga, he could not believe his own eyes.

'Maranga, no. Can't be. Yes, it's you. Grace, come and see Lewis. He is here! He is here!'

'Bethwell, I got out of jail today. Do you still keep my things? I want us to put all the important things in one box. Hurry, let's get going. And if anybody asks you whether I was here tonight, tell them that you never saw me. Tell them that I am still in jail.'

This story did not make any sense to Bethwell Mbarathi. But that was not important now. What mattered was to help a friend in need. The big box was filled up with all sorts of things.

' 'Bye for now. Will be seeing you.'

Bethwell Mbarathi was a very puzzled gentleman. All this looked like a nasty dream. One moment there was Lewis. The next moment there was no Lewis. Like a jack-in-the-box.

Kalule now drove the van to Hotel Olivia. He was careful not to park the vehicle too close to the hotel entrance. The two boxes were removed. Maranga was asked to go to the hotel and book three rooms. The van was now driven to a lonely spot near the Railway Station where it was left. The only thing Kalule took from the prison van was Warder Wambua's bunch of keys. He left everything else in that van, including his medical kit. Kalule and Menja now walked back to the hotel. Maranga had already booked the necessary rooms.

At Hotel Olivia they are very polite. You book in, you are given a room and you can stay there for as long as you want. But of course you must remember to pay on your last day. And if that is not a polite way of going about things, I don't know what is.

The newspapers the following morning were full of juicy stories. The radio told the story of the prison van in glowing terms. That a prison warder and a prison driver were found asleep in a prison van. That they were wearing prison clothes and that they were both handcuffed. That bottles of chloroform were found in the van. That the sleeping gentlemen were taken to the hospital where they later regained consciousness. That nevertheless the two had lost their memory and that the story which they told on gaining consciousness was incoherent and unintelligible. That the whole thing was a great mystery but investigations were continuing.

But the escape was not mentioned. The papers and the radio did not say anything about the three prisoners who escaped. Maybe this information was being withheld so as not to hamper investigations.

That same morning, Kalule and Maranga sent messengers from Hotel Olivia to cash cheques for them. They would not venture out for fear of detection. When the money came, they paid off their bills. They put the rest of the money in their pockets. It was a lot of money.

Then came a sad farewell. Time had come for Menja Kihara to go his way. He told his two friends where he was going and he said that he hoped that they would visit him one day.

Kalule and Maranga went in the next Peugeot taxi to Eldoret. From there they planned to disappear into Uganda. It is not a good practice to leave money lying idle in a bank. Maybe by now somebody would have told them up there at Kampala that Yowasi Kizito cannot sign a cheque.

A big meeting was held at Kabete Jail on the morning following the escape. The jail commandant was in the chair. Chief Inspector Noel Kimamo was there. Superintendent Kahiu Kimotho was there too. There was a lot of other top brass at this meeting.

Angry words were exchanged. Charges of inefficiency were levelled at some officers. The news media also came in for some criticism for dramatising the case.

The prison commandant was angry, annoyed, afraid. Angry because his staff had let him down. Annoyed because of the way it had happened. Afraid because the keys which were taken from Warder Wambua were very important keys. If these keys were not found, the commandant would definitely lose his job. Lots of other officers would be fired as well.

All because one key in that bunch is the key to the armoury. Inside that armoury, there were lots of guns. Lots of machine guns. Lots of ammunition. Lots of other fighting equipment. Not prison stuff, no. This is army stuff, hidden inside a prison. The army does not keep all its armaments in the army barracks, if you didn't know. They hide them in one or two other places. That's how you beat the enemy, by hiding your fighting equipment in the most unlikely of places. Such as Kabete Jail. That's why those keys that Kalule has got are so important. That's why somebody must get those keys back.

And why should Warder Wambua be carrying such an important bunch of keys with him? It's another security trick. Everybody imagines that all the important keys are carried by the jail commandant. In case of trouble, this would be the man to go for. But no, there are still some clever people left on this earth. You must fool the enemy. That's why the keys are carried by somebody else, a junior officer in the place, but a trusted officer all the same.

But Warder Wambua did not know that he was carrying an armoury key with him. His instructions were that those keys were only to be given to two army officers in case of need. The two army officers would identify themselves by saying some secret words which Warder Wambua knew. It was an elaborate system but it was reliable. But Kalule has now spoiled it all by washing Warder Wambua with a good dose of chloroform. What a pity!

The big meeting came out with one resolution. It was directed at Superintendent Kahiu Kimotho of the Kenya Police. He was commanded to do everything in his power to get those keys back. He was empowered to do anything he chose to. He was asked to forget everything else and to concentrate on those keys only.

'We are giving you this task, Superintendent, because you know two of the three prisoners. You know their ways, their whims, their weaknesses. We are giving you full freedom to negotiate for the return of those keys. Do what you think is best.'

Superintendent Kimotho nodded in assent. The senior officer representing the police ended the meeting on a sweet note.

'Superintendent Kimotho, promotion awaits you if you bring us back those keys.' The Superintendent liked that part.

But this was a difficult job. Where do you start on a job like this? Supposing somebody just threw those keys out into the bush, or into a river, or into a pit latrine? Just where do you start?

Well, by contacting Jane Njeri. By looking for the minister's daughter. This was the one and only person who knew both Kalule and Maranga. This was the person who helped to throw these two people into jail in the first place. She was the only person who could be used as a contact after finding out where Kalule and Maranga were hiding. But there was one problem. Where was Jane Njeri herself?

Superintendent Kimotho made a beeline for the bank.

'Is Jane Njeri still working here?'

'No, she resigned almost three years ago. We don't know where she went to.'

That's disappointing, isn't it. What about her flat on Latema Road? Maybe they have some information about Njeri there. Superintendent Kimotho goes there. There is a new tenant in the place. It is a young man who looks like a student. He has long, unkempt hair. His eyes are flashing from side to side as if the poor fellow has just been reading about the habits of the chameleon.

'Who was here before you?'

'A big fat man with a great long beard.'

'And who was here before the big fat man?'

'Ask the big fat man that question.'

'Where is the big fat man himself?'

'I don't know. That's a stupid question to ask, Mister.'

The chap banged the door with a very loud noise and disappeared into the small room. For one fleeting moment, Superintendent Kimotho thought that he would rather find himself face to face with a spitting cobra than with this type of humanity.

How disappointing. Who else knows anything about Jane Njeri? There was that girl we took down to Mombasa. Her name was Eunice Wangeci. But where is Eunice now? Nobody knows. How disappointing.

Back to the bank.

'Have you got Jane Njeri's record? The name of her home area, for example? The name of her next of kin, for example?'

'Yes, we have. She came from a place called Ihithe in the Nyeri District. Her father's name is Absalom Gacara, a clergyman. Is that enough, Superintendent?'

'Yes, it is.'

How nice, how nice. Tomorrow we go to Ihithe. We shall look for Absalom Gacara, the clergyman. Maybe he knows where his daughter is. If he doesn't, we shall have to call it off as a bad job. And if somebody attacks, we shall have to dynamite Kabete Jail to get at those guns. Not a very civilised thing to do, is it?

Superintendent Kimotho was at Nyeri the following day. He booked in at the 'Black Leopard', this new place which cropped up recently next to the Roman Catholic Cathedral. That same day he drove up to Ihithe school. The roads to that place were bumpy and full of potholes. But the countryside was a beauty to behold. Steep hills and green valleys. Fast little streams full of clear, cold water. Life here went on in a slow, methodical way, as if nobody was in any hurry to get to anywhere. The only thing that was sometimes in some sort of a hurry was the cool wind. It chilled your ears and made the fingers numb.

When he got to Ihithe school, Superintendent Kimotho spoke to the very first person he came across. There was something modern about this man. He even had a necktie. A very tight necktie, a torn coat and baggy trousers.

'Good morning. You live here, I presume?'

'Live here? What do you mean? I was born here. I will surely die here. Are you the Education Officer at Nyeri? Might you be the person who transfers teachers from one place to another?'

'No, my name is Superintendent Kimotho of the Kenya Police.'

'I am Teacher Andrew Karanja of the Kenya Teaching Service. We haven't had any murders here for the past eighteen years. We have no robberies here either. What would a whole Superintendent like you be coming here for?'

'I am looking for a certain Absalom Gacara. He is a clergy-man.'

'Goodness gracious me! What has he done? If there is anybody in this place who hasn't done anything evil it's him. He doesn't drink, he doesn't smoke, he doesn't do anything. Why do you want to see him?'

'If you want to know, he is the father of a girl called Jane Njeri.'

'That's what you think, Kimotho, but we all know the truth now. Let's go, I will show you Gacara's home. His house is just beyond the school.'

They now began walking slowly towards the school compound. Kimotho made sure that they did not walk too fast because he wanted to know one or two things from this talkative teacher.

'Do you mean to tell me, Teacher Karanja, that Gacara is not Njeri's father?'

'I will leave you to find that out for yourself. But it is not usual for people to adopt children if they can have some of their own.'

'Was Jane Njeri adopted?'

'No, she was the daughter of her mother Agatha. But this other boy that they got the other day is adopted.'

Kimotho was not really interested in all this. What he wanted to know was Jane's whereabouts.

'Has anybody here at Ihithe seen Jane Njeri recently?'

'Gacara will tell you that.'

'Do you know when she left home to go to Nairobi?'

'Gacara will tell you that.'

The teacher was proving difficult to handle, and so Kimotho decided not to ask any more direct questions.

Before long they came to Absalom Gacara's home. Bwana Absalom was there and his wife Agatha was preparing lunch. They went into the house. Bwana Absalom came to meet them.

'Bwana Absalom,' the teacher said, 'meet Inspector Kimotho of the Kenya C.I.D. These are the people who catch criminals. I understand he wants to catch Jane Njeri for something or other.'

When Agatha heard the name of her daughter mentioned, she emerged from the kitchen in a hurry. She was introduced to Kimotho by the teacher. Kimotho felt rather embarrassed to be called an inspector with the C.I.D.

'I am Superintendent, not Inspector,' he said.

'That's a more senior rank than Inspector, Bwana Absalom,' the teacher said. 'It means that the matter is even more serious than I thought. A whole Superintendent? I have never seen one in my whole life.'

'Further,' Kimotho continued, 'I am not here to catch anybody or anything like that. I am not investigating any crime.'

'And you expect us to believe that, do you?' The teacher held his mouth to hold back his sinister laughter.

'Teacher Karanja,' Gacara said, 'it is obvious that something serious has happened. But Kimotho is now our guest, not yours. Will you allow us to talk to him? Will everybody sit down please?'

Everybody sat down around the table. The Bwana was now determined to take command of the situation.

'Superintendent Kimotho, what is your other name?' he asked.

'Kahiu. That is my first name,' he said.

'Is that all? Haven't you got a Christian name?'

'I really don't know. Maybe I had one when I was a child, but nobody ever told me about it when I grew up. But is this important?'

'No, I just wanted to know.'

This was not going to be a good day for Absalom Gacara. Maybe his daughter had killed somebody. To make matters worse, they send a heathen to investigate. Still, Bwana Absalom hoped that things were not quite as bad as that.

'You are our guest, Kimotho,' he said. 'According to tradition, you will first rest and eat. After that, you will tell us why you came to see us.'

Agatha now left the group and went back to the kitchen. She was frying very good 'irio'. The leeks at Ihithe are thick and long. She cut one into small pieces and put them into the frying pan. She then added cooking fat and went on with the rest of the job. There has never been any doubt about the quality of Agatha's cooking.

Back at the table, the conversation now centred on the weather. The Bwana was propounding a theory on how the whole world is getting more and more dry and how one day rain will disappear altogether. He talked in earnest of how, long ago, there used to be lightning and thunder for days on end during the rainy season. These days one would be lucky to hear one tiny roar in six months, he said.

Bwana Absalom cut short his speech when a small boy entered the house. The boy had a writing case with him, and appeared to have come from school. He was also in school uniform.

Kimotho held the boy by the hand and asked him, 'What is your name, little boy?'

'Joshua Abednego Mathai. And what is your name?'

'His name is Superintendent Kimotho,' the teacher said. 'He is here to catch all the naughty boys.' The teacher held his mouth again to hold off his laughter.

'Where does he come from?' the boy asked.

'He is from Nairobi. Do you want to go with him to Nairobi?' the teacher asked.

'Yes,' the boy answered.

'No, son,' the Bwana said. 'Nairobi is a very big place. It is not like Ihithe. You can easily get lost there.'

Kimotho was not talking. He was looking at this boy. Kimotho could recognise faces easily and he was quick to note likenesses. This was part of his job as a policeman. He could not fail to note the way this boy resembled Jane Njeri. There was no doubt in his mind whatsoever that this boy's facial features and a good deal of his behaviour resembled those of the girl he was looking for.

Kimotho did not mention this resemblance to anybody. Maybe it was all superficial, maybe it was a mere coincidence. But he decided there and then to find out more about this boy. It would not be difficult for him to find out the boy's background from the Adoption Society of Kenya.

Lunch came. Kimotho was about to start eating when he felt something peculiar in the air. Everybody was staring at their food, but nobody was eating it. Before long, he found out why.

'Oh Lord,' the Bwana said, closing his eyes, 'bless this food that you have so kindly placed before us. May we cherish this gift that you have given us although we are sinners. Guide our steps this day and always so that we may not put others into trouble, that we may leave in peace what we found in peace. Give your divine guidance to our guest here today, so that he does not ruin the lives of old people on their last days here on earth. Above all, Oh Lord, guide our lips, especially the lips of the teachers and the womenfolk among us, so that our lips and our tongues will not utter words which do not have your approval. Praise to thee, Oh Lord, for ever and ever.'

The others, save Kimotho, said in unison, 'Amen.'

The food was good, very good indeed. Then everybody had a cup of tea. It wasn't really tea but milk adulterated with a little tea. There are lots of grade cattle at Ihithe and they produce a lot of milk.

After the meal, Bwana Absalom faced Kimotho and began talking to him.

'Now, Kimotho, tell us what crime has been committed.'

'None whatsoever, Bwana Absalom. I do not investigate crimes. That is done by my junior officers.'

'What do you do then? Why have you come to Ihithe?'

'I investigate people. According to Government records, your daughter Jane Njeri has not been here for seven years, isn't that so?'

'Yes.'

'We are concerned that she has not been here to see her parents for such a long time.'

Everybody now kept quiet, but not for long. Agatha had something to say.

'Are you sure that our daughter has not been involved in any crime?'

'Yes, certainly,' Kimotho said.

'All you want is to find out why she has not been here, is that so?'

'Not quite. I would like to be instrumental in bringing her back to you. I am sure you would be pleased to see her, wouldn't you?'

'We would, certainly,' Agatha said. 'How can we help you do it?'

'Simple. Tell me where she is now.'

Agatha disappeared into the bedroom and came back with a letter. Bwana Absalom looked at his wife disapprovingly. He was not quite sure whether Agatha was doing the right thing. Agatha gave this letter to Kimotho.

'Read that,' she said. 'It will tell you where Njeri is.'

The letter was headed 'Kitui Women's Teacher Training College'. That was enough.

'Thank you very much,' Kimotho said. 'I very much appreciate your help.'

'When do we see our daughter, then?' Bwana Absalom asked.

'In less than a month, I should think.'

Kimotho went back to his car and drove down to Nyeri. It was a downhill drive all the way. He was happy that he was now getting somewhere at long last.

After Kimotho left, the folks at Ihithe kept talking.

'I don't trust that man,' the teacher said.

'I don't either,' Absalom agreed. 'Have you ever heard of policemen who roam about the country bringing children back to their parents? That is not the work of the police.'

The only person who appeared to trust Kimotho was Agatha.

'So long as he brings back our daughter to us,' she said, 'I shall be happy.'

'Still,' the teacher added, 'I will be surprised if she hasn't committed a major crime all those years she has been in Nairobi.'

They decided to wait. Waiting is not a problem at Ihithe. At any rate, what other alternative was there?

When Kimotho got back to Nairobi, his first duty was to contact the Adoption Society of Kenya. He explained to them the nature of his mission and requested them to furnish him with the information he wanted.

His suspicion was correct. The little boy whom Bwana Absalom and his wife Agatha had adopted was their daughter's son. Kimotho now recalled what Jane Njeri had told him a long time ago when he was investigating Ali Kamau's murder. It was all very intriguing.

Jane Njeri had been at Kitui Women's Teacher Training College for the last three years or so. At this college, she had at last found the peace of mind that she so desperately needed.

To Njeri, peace of mind was a new experience, a welcome experience, an experience she was determined to make a permanent feature of her life.

She had also come to like teaching as a career and she had made up her mind to be a teacher for the rest of her life.

She was happy that she had succeeded at last in running away from a life of crime. She was now a mature girl, she was a grown-up woman, she was now in a position to look back on her own life with a mature mind, something she could not have done before coming to this College.

Jane spent many sleepless nights trying to look back on her own life. There was no doubt in her mind that her upbringing had been narrow and one-sided, that she did not grow up like many of her friends did. Her religious upbringing was meant to instil in her a firm moral discipline. It was supposed to give her a foundation based on righteousness. Sadly, this foundation never took root.

Something must have gone wrong somewhere. Although she was a victim of circumstances on many occasions, Jane was now mature enough to accept that she was to blame for a good deal of what had happened to her and others. She was to blame because she had allowed herself, willingly, to participate directly in crime. The fact that she was the person who put poison into Ali Kamau's drink kept haunting her day and night.

But Jane was now ready to let the past bury its dead. She had firmly resolved to be a different person now, a person with clean hands. No more would she allow herself to be used as an accomplice. Never again was she going to associate with people whom she knew were involved in crime.

The fact that Jane still knew nothing about her child was a bitter

176

pill to swallow. Maybe when she had finished her training, she would think of ways of trying to find out where her child was. She knew that she might never find out about her child, but she had now decided not to get into crime again because of this. She was convinced that every problem has a solution, a clean solution. To maintain her sanity and peace of mind, Jane decided to do what is right, irrespective of the circumstances. After all, she was still young and she was still capable of having more children.

This was her last term and she had just finished her final examinations. The results would be out within two days. Then there would be a graduation ceremony. After this, the girls would go home to await instructions on where each teacher would be posted.

On the last day of school the headmistress called Jane Njeri to her office.

'There is a tall boy here who calls himself Kahiu Kimotho. He wants to see you. Do you know him?'

'Yes, Madam. I knew him a long time ago. He is a Superintendent of Police.'

'I suspected he was a policeman the moment I saw him, Jane. Now, why does he want to see you? Jane, have you done anything ... I want to hear the truth.'

'No, nothing at all, Madam.'

'Then I will call him in, but let me do all the talking. Do you understand?'

Kimotho was now called into the office. He shook Jane's hand very warmly.

'You know each other then, Kimotho?'

'Yes. We met in Nairobi three years ago.'

'Please take a seat. May I know what you do?'

'I am a policeman, Madam. I am a Superintendent in the Kenya Police.'

'I see, I see. And what can we do for you, Superintendent?'

'Nothing much, only that I want to take Njeri away from you. She helped me to investigate a forgery and a murder and I am certain that she will be equally useful to me now.'

'Did you say forgery and murder? Was she involved?'

'Yes, she was. But we had a good reason to let her go.'

The headmistress virtually collapsed on her desk. She really wasn't expecting to hear this. How can a beautiful, obedient and intelligent girl like Njeri get mixed up with forgery and murder?

'So you want to take her away then, Superintendent?'

'Yes.'

'We were going to close the College tomorrow anyhow and I do not think that I have any objection.'

Jane Njeri packed up her things and said good-bye to her friends in a hurry. She would miss the graduation ceremony, but the Education Officer at Nyeri would be informed of her grades. He would then decide where to post her.

The road from Kitui to Nairobi is very dusty and is also full of corrugations. And the buses, those buses. After one passes you, you see nothing but a thick cloud of dust for a whole minute. At times Kimotho had to come to a halt altogether rather than drive on into an invisible road. Apart from the dust, however, the journey was quite good and Kimotho kept Njeri engaged in a conversation all the way.

'Sorry to pull you out of your graduation ceremony, Jane, but I have a very tough job on my hands right now.'

'What's the trouble now, Kimotho?'

Kimotho told Njeri all about the big escape. He then told her that he wanted her to help him to bring these culprits to justice.

'And why me in particular?' she asked.

'Because you know both of them well. It will not be difficult for you to talk to them, to gain their confidence.'

'Why do you want me to talk to them? Surely if you know where these people are, you can have them arrested at once.'

'We don't know where they are Jane, that's the first problem. The second problem is that not only are we interested in these rogues, we are also interested in what they are carrying.'

Kimotho now told Njeri about those keys. She listened very attentively, but she could not quite seem to believe in this story.

'So you see, Jane, it would be a great pity if we arrested these people and found out that they did not have those keys with them.'

'So what do you want me to do?'

'As soon as we know where they are, I want you to go to them, talk to them, stay with them and find out whether they have those keys.'

'And then?'

'Let me know so that I can arrest them.'

Jane Njeri was now convinced that crime does not pay and so she was ready to help Kimotho in every possible way. It did not matter to her whether Lewis Maranga was her childhood friend or whether Donald Kalule held the secret of her child. She had already made up her mind on the sort of life she wanted to live and nothing would change that decision.

'O.K., Kimotho,' she said. 'I will do what you want.'

When they got to Nairobi, Jane was booked in at a good hotel. Kimotho went to his office on Tom Mboya Street and called his commanding officer Assistant Commissioner Morris Mrefu on the line.

'The girl is now in Nairobi, sir.'

'Is she willing to help us?'

'Very much so, sir.'

'I am afraid, Kimotho, we may not need her help.'

'Why?'

'Our boys have done a wonderful job. They know where two of the three escapees are.'

'Where?'

'At the "Black Leopard" in Nyeri, that's where. All that we need to do now is to arrest them in a calm, cool manner.'

'And the keys? They may not have them.'

'They have.' The proprietor did a little homework for us. He saw the keys with his own eyes. The excitement is over, Kimotho, I am afraid. I shall leave you to arrest them when you want.'

Kimotho now called Jane at her hotel.

'Jane,' he said, 'I am sure you could do with a little rest.'

'By tomorrow morning I will have had all the rest I need, Kimotho.'

'I want to give you two full days in which to do nothing.'

'But I came here to do something, didn't I?'

'The picture has changed a little, Jane, so you take a rest until I call you again. But I am unlikely to require your services for another forty-eight hours, so you can go round the city and do some shopping.'

The following morning, Kimotho drove all the way to Nyeri and met the proprietor of the 'Black Leopard' in a farmhouse on the other side of the Nyeri Hill.

'Let me first thank you for helping us out in this difficult job,' Kimotho said. 'I want to arrest the two people the day after tomorrow.' Then Kimotho explained in detail how he wanted this done.

The proprietor did not like Kimotho's plan. He was afraid that his hotel might get a bad name if it came to be known that two criminals had sought refuge there.

'Is there no way of arresting them without bringing my hotel into disrepute?' he asked.

Kimotho thought for a while. His friend had a good point. If the other hotel residents came to know that they were rubbing shoulders with dangerous criminals, they might feel obliged to book out and seek for alternative accommodation.

Kimotho left for Nairobi without having made any definite plan as to how he would arrest Maranga and Kalule without disrupting the normal life at the hotel. The only way he could think of was to enter their rooms in the small hours of the morning and take them. But then things might not turn out to be quite so simple. Nobody knew whether these two were armed. Kimotho had to think about other alternatives.

By lunchtime on the following day, Kimotho had a plan, a good plan. In the afternoon, he went over to Jane Njeri's hotel and they discussed this plan. It was a very simple plan and he was surprised that he had not thought of it before. The arrest was planned to take place the following day, which would be a Saturday, in the afternoon.

At about half past two that Saturday, Jane Njeri walked into the 'Black Leopard' and went and sat in the bar. A waiter came to her in a few minutes and she asked for a soft drink. Then she looked round. There were little groups of people here and there but there was nobody she could recognise.

Nobody recognised her either. But she knew that before long, the two fugitives would be coming down to see her. The hotel proprietor would see to that.

Jane knew that Superintendent Kahiu Kimotho was within the vicinity of the hotel. She also knew that Acting Superintendent Geoffrey Kiptanui was hiding around the corner somewhere with a company of his Haraka Specials just in case he was needed. Nobody was taking any chances on this job. Those keys must go back to their owners, and those two fugitives must go back to prison. Maybe when they are back behind bars they will tell the authorities where their colleague Mwenja Kihara is.

But Jane knew something else too. She knew that she was going to be instrumental in bringing about a successful arrest. The part that she would play would be small but vital. She was happy that she had accepted to play this part if only to prove to herself that she was ready to turn her back on crime.

At about three o'clock, the receptionist went upstairs and knocked at room number fifteen.

'Yes?' Maranga called.

'A visitor for you.'

'For me? What visitor?'

'A woman called Jane Njeri. She wants to see both Kalule and yourself. She is waiting downstairs. Please don't keep her waiting for long.' The receptionist left.

Maranga went into the next room, which was Kalule's. He told him about the visitor waiting for them downstairs.

'Can't be, Maranga. Somebody must be going mad without

realizing it,' Kalule said. 'I am sure they saw somebody else, not Jane Njeri.'

'You could be right, Kalule, and you could be wrong. But just supposing Njeri is waiting for us downstairs. What would you suggest we do?'

'There are two ways. Either we go down and see her or we don't.'

'And what's your way, Kalule? Me, I don't feel like going down to see this girl. It is in my nature not to trust women.'

'Me, I trust them, Maranga, especially when you have a secret which the woman wants to know. I have a secret which this girl wants to know. I will tell you about that later.'

Donald Kalule was convinced that Jane Njeri had come to see him about her child. He had no doubts about that. But he decided not to tell her anything about it until she told him how she knew where they were hiding. He would also want to know from her whether they were safe, and if not, whether she could help them to look for another hiding place. Kalule definitely wanted to see Njeri. She had helped him before and he was sure she would help him again.

'Are you coming, Maranga?' Kalule asked.

'No. You go down first.'

Kalule went downstairs into the bar. He had no difficulty in recognising Jane. He went straight to her and they shook hands Kalule sat down opposite her and ordered a beer.

'I am certainly very glad to see you after three years or more, Jane,' Kalule said. 'How did you know we were here?'

'I will tell you, Kalule, but first tell me where Maranga is,' she said.

'Upstairs, but he is not feeling well.'

Jane now told the doctor about herself and how she had gone into teaching. The doctor in turn talked about his trial and how he was sent to jail.

'But they had no real proof on me, and so they sent me to jail for three years only,' he said.

'I am very relieved to hear that, Kalule,' Jane said. 'Friends of mine have been telling me that you people escaped from prison and that the police were looking for you. I am very glad to hear that this is not the case.'

Kalule's mouth went dry all of a sudden. Droplets of sweat gathered on his forehead and his heart was thumping irregularly inside his chest as if it was overheating.

'What did your friends tell you, Jane?' he asked. 'Tell me everything and I will tell you everything you want to know.'

Jane was now seized with a great temptation to ask about her child. She tried to resist the urge but she just could not hold herself back.

'Kalule,' she said, 'there is one thing you have never told me. You remember . . .'

'I remember, Jane, I do. But tell me about what your friends told you about us first,' he said. Kalule knew that he held the trump card, and he was not going to let off his secret for nothing.

Jane made up her mind there and then not to ask about her child again. This was not part of the plan, and she had promised herself that she would not allow herself to be distracted from the path she had chosen.

'I have already told you what people have told me about you two,' she said. 'In fact, this is why I came here. Plenty of people know where both of you are hiding. You see, somebody told me in confidence that the police were coming to arrest you tomorrow. So I thought of coming here to let you know that you are not as safe as you probably think. I would suggest that you book out immediately and go to some other place.'

Kalule acted at once. He asked Njeri to go and call a taxi. A taxi came, with a Haraka Specials corporal disguised as the driver. Kalule and Maranga booked out of the 'Black Leopard' and got into this taxi. That night, the two went back to jail.

As soon as the taxi drove off Kimotho stormed into the hotel and sat next to Jane. He congratulated her quietly and asked for a cold beer. Everything had gone according to plan. Nobody in the hotel knew what was going on, nobody was disturbed.

'And now, Jane,' Kimotho said, 'I will do my last duty of the day. I will drive you to your home at Ihithe. I am sure your parents will be glad to see you.'

Kimotho took the Kamakwa road. Before long he was at Mununga, heading west towards Ihithe.

'Jane,' he said, 'you are very quiet. What's the matter?'

'Nothing much. Only that I have now come of age.'

'What do you mean?'

'I would not have turned those two people over to you if I had been what I was three years ago.'

'Keep your hands clean and you will always be happy,' Kimotho counselled.

Then a long pause. Neither of them appeared to be ready to talk but Kimotho thought he had better say something.

'You did your job well, Jane, and you will be well rewarded. What reward do you want?'

'Peace of mind,' she said.

'I can't give you that. It's only you who can give yourself that reward. But maybe I can give you the next best thing.'

'No, Kimotho. I don't want any money. I will be in employment from next month onwards.'

'I am not thinking of money, Jane. What you have done deserves a better reward than that.'

They now came to a junction. Kimotho took the right turning, the one that goes to the left, towards Kigogo. Jane was rather surprised to see that Kimotho knew the right way.

'You seem to know the way,' Jane said.

'Yes. I have been at Ihithe before.'

'What were you doing there?'

He explained. Jane listened with her mouth open.

'Are you ready to accept my reward now, Jane?'

'Yes. Let me hear what it is.'